# THE IMMANENCE OF

# GOD IN THE TROPICS

Also by George Rosen

*Black Money: A Novel of Modern Africa*

Stories

# The Immanence of God in the Tropics

George Rosen

*Leapfrog Press*
*Fredonia, New York*

Published in 2012 in the United States by
Leapfrog Press LLC
PO Box 505
Fredonia, NY 14063
www.leapfrogpress.com

Printed in the United States of America

Distributed in the United States by
Consortium Book Sales and Distribution
St. Paul, Minnesota 55114
www.cbsd.com

Author photo by Barbara Gale

Cover image © 2012 Banco de México Diego Rivera Frida Kahlo
Museums Trust, Mexico, D.F. / Artists Rights Society (ARS), New York

First Edition

Library of Congress Cataloging-in-Publication Data

Rosen, George H., 1946-
  The immanence of God in the Tropics / George Rosen.
-- 1st ed.
    p. cm.
  ISBN 978-1-935248-31-6
  1. Voyages and travels--Fiction. 2. Travelers--Fiction. 3.  Short stories.
I. Title.
  PS3568.O7649I55 2012
  813'.54--dc23


    2012031013

For Barbara, again

For Sam and Daniel, for the first time

For Harold, Roslyn, and Marc, from the beginning

# Contents

# Kenya, 1973

## Our Big Game

My students were dissecting field mice when Gichuru called me into the school office. Gichuru is our headmaster, an intelligent man with a dark, handsome African face that belongs on a coin. He waved a letter in my face. "Read it!" he said. "They refuse to come here. He says our field is like a battleground, that if the game is played here the boys will disappear into holes, that they will never be seen again."

I looked at MacIntyre's letter. It indeed said those things, and more—insinuations about safari ants (which had some truth to them) and quicksand (which were ridiculous). The school where I teach is small. It is quite new, built after Independence, and it is poor, without money to pay for glass windows or concrete sidewalks. The soccer field does in fact have a rise in the middle which can partially obscure oncoming players and there are a few potholes hidden by high grass. They are not "deep and perilous" as MacIntyre's letter claimed.

But MacIntyre has a bee up his ass about our school

and especially about our headmaster. Gichuru was once a student of his, an exemplary prefect whom MacIntyre permitted to wear long pants. But now that they are in positions of nominal equality, MacIntyre detests him. "Detests" is probably too gentle a term for the loathing MacIntyre feels. He places on Gichuru's shoulders the blame for all that has gone awry in East Africa in the past forty years, all the crevasses and faults that have crumbled Mac's now queasy firmament.

Gichuru does not deserve this. He is a conscientious, perennially worried man who would be better off if he had even one-half the demonic energy Mac attributes to him. Basically clerkish, Gichuru has immense respect for the written word. He issues frequent memoranda to students, cutting elegant stencils for our mimeograph machine. He admires files and keeps too many old letters. Far from being an avenger of old injustices, he is—or would be, but for a solid core of dignity—a sycophant of peace and quiet.

His office is small, a corrugated tin cubicle sliced off the end of a long block of classrooms. One cannot storm about in it. But even seated at his desk, Gichuru was still furious. Furious and hurt. He knew that our field was not what it should be and that Mac's—graded, damped, chalked, and dusted into a pampered baby of a field—was better. But it was an issue of pride and proper alternation.

I suggested a neutral site, the coffee research station ten miles from us, neatly between the two schools and

run by a neutral party. Abraham Muriuki is also a former student of Mac's, a knightly scientist-scholar who
has read widely in his evenings up there on the mountain and understands things foreign to East Africa, like
the Abominable Snowman and Huey Long, as well as
he knows the secrets of the Chinese box of husks and
shells in which the coffee bean lies. The research station has a soccer field, too, neither so elegant as Mac's
nor so humble as our own. Gichuru sent me off after
class to present the plan to MacIntyre.

I had intended to go up the road anyway to see Sally.
She teaches at the girls' school that forms a part—although a more remote part than the boys' school—of
Mac's complex of powers at Chorumbe. I rode in the
back of a Land Rover taxi between bags of black millet
and clumps of chickens tied together at the feet. Everywhere on the road there were runners: boys and
girls in school uniforms, policemen in their military
caps and khaki shorts. The whole country has gone
mad for running, especially those who have read the
papers and seen the Olympians, their pictures wired
from Mexico City and Munich: Kipchoge with the
medals around his neck, a sombrero on his head, his
smile as wide as a feeding whale's. Children who used
to run from house to house in the morning juggling a
hot coal in their hands to bring fire to a neighbor, now
do it all for sport. They measure off the mountainside
into 1500-meter chunks, and errands take half-time.
The primary kids come to school early, are home before

dark, and off again on the road, lamps in their hands, the earth spinning underfoot.

But MacIntyre stands still. He arranges the motion of others. At our school, if students quarrel, they must settle their differences before nightfall; if two fight, both are punished. Equilibrium is the goal. At Mac's school he makes them box, whether the quarrel was peaceful or violent. They are not used to the gloves. At no other time do they fight this way. But Mac makes them circle and strike with all of their running quadrangled off until one falls down. Then the others must watch while MacIntyre raises a hand in victory and dismisses them all to the dormitory. Even there, while the students run among the cots and the piled exercise books, they know that Mac may be near, still and watching. He has been known to stand just beyond the windows during the study period that precedes sleep, listening to make sure that all their talking is in English. If he hears a phrase in Kigeli or an oath—and the oaths will be in Kigeli, for all their English has been learned from him and they have been given no words for hostility or despair—then he bursts in. He comes so suddenly that there seems to be no door or steps, nothing except the apparition of Mac, his bald head like a great marble egg boring up through the tamped dirt floor, dragging the speakers of forbidden utterances off to punishment.

The man has no flesh. He is all stone and bone. Even under an equatorial sun in a short-sleeved shirt and corduroy shorts he stays white as a sepulchre. He wears a hat, though, a large, perfect cone of straw in the style of the country in which he was born—Basutoland, which is now called Lesotho—a mountain enclave in south Africa where his parents were missionaries. The family trails missionaries back for generation upon generation. Mac is pure, untainted by memory. He has none of the sullen escapism of the runaway missionaries who have left modest positions at home and come out for the servants and deference as much as for the challenge of the faithless, those who still remember snow and marigolds and the friendly anonymity of being roughly the same color as everyone else.

But like a sailor who has known only captains, seamen, prostitutes, and fish, the world for Mac is peopled in skewed and perplexing ways. He sees no whites between the ages of five and twenty since the children of other missionaries are all whisked away to schools in England, America, or Nairobi. Blackness, for Mac, is a condition of adolescence like acne or daydreams, a forcing-house through which dark and light babies pass according to a scheme over which he himself presides.

When I arrived at Chorumbe, Sally was in her front room grading papers. Out her window I could see Mac by the soccer field at the top of the ridge. He stood tall with his cone hat, still and straight, while the afternoon sun flattened the scurrying football squads into two clashing lines. MacIntyre's soccer teams never lose except through minor epidemics or treachery. Even when some of the players are three-quarters of the way to a malarial crisis there is no guarantee of defeat. One of Mac's front lines—their brains and brows inflamed with fever—can speed down the field like the wall of a burning forest, scorching everything before them. The first tiers of the opposition curl and cinder to ash, then the backs, until nothing lies between the goalie and his destruction but the ball, afire like Mac's will with a heat so intense that it consumes the flesh. It touches and will burn right through the goalie's grasp into the net, leaving nothing at the end of the goalkeeper's arms but faint outlines—the merest memory of human hands.

Sally told me she thought of seducing Mac last month.

"Blackmail?"

"Oh come on. Humiliation. Compromise. Can you imagine what would happen if Mac was discovered making midnight advances on Chorumbe's one unmarried white woman in the privacy of her bedchamber? It would be such a relief to everyone. The old women would sing. It would be wonderful!"

"What was he doing in your bedchamber at midnight?"

"Changing the light bulb."

MacIntyre conserves energy. The generator shed is

next to his house and the machine runs only from dusk to one a.m. Mac has all the light bulbs. He doesn't approve of high wattage and everyone's eyes tear for his thrift. If a bulb fails, the teacher (it will not be a student since they cannot leave their dormitory after dinner time) must plead at MacIntyre's door like the Holy Roman Emperor who abased himself in the snow before the pope's mountain retreat. Then Mac will come with his bag of light.

Sally had been reading *The Prisoner of Zenda* in bed when the light went out and she stumbled down the path to Mac's house in only her raincoat and underwear. Mac came out to her in boots and his immense wool nightshirt. No one ever remembers a time when Mac did not wear it on his late night calls. It must have grown up with him, some anonymous Basuto hands weaving it taller as the boy grew until now it has the age and majesty of something fit to be found in a pharoah's tomb.

It occurred to Sally that there was a quality of knightliness about Mac—white-gowned and bulb-clutching as he was—something in his single-pointed determination to pursue the consequences of his power. As they crossed the threshold into Sally's house, now darker than the moonlit forest behind it, this knightliness—and the light—gave their actions a medieval cast and made it a kind of elopement.

For a moment she entertained the thought of exploring the issue, of testing him. But there was nothing really to explore. He refused the cup of tea by candle-light which Sally offered, and while feudal romances flickered briefly in her brain against all knowledge of the man, Mac, oblivious, changed the light. He stood on her bed and strained for the dangling socket. When the new bulb finally shone, he looked down at this lovely woman in her raincoat and underwear and saw nothing but a skeleton. Her womanness to him was a few extra centimeters of pelvic girdle—just bones—our mortal lattice staring up his nightshirt.

"He told me to do my reading by daylight. I could have stripped and it wouldn't have meant a thing to him. He'd rather eat his apples and be severe."

Sally gave her sympathies about the game. As she realized, there was a question of money in all this—the rental of a vehicle to ferry our team back and forth to the research station—something we could barely afford every other year in the normal course of things. And there was a failed obligation to our fans—the other students and their families who would all have come if we'd played at home, the old women cheer-ing their grandsons on as if the President had come to town. Mac couldn't care less about the money. He owned his own bus and could bring whomever he pleased. Against his host we would have only Mugam-bi (our school watchman and owner of the Land Rover we would rent), Gichuru, and myself.

Sally was right about the apples. Mac was chewing on one when I talked with him. He has them shipped in from Kitale in the Rift Valley, the only place in the country where they grow. These are equatorial apples—too rosy and soft. Their texture is to the real fruit's as sausage is to steak. Mac supplies his own crunch. He didn't object to our scheme. Any location, he said, would suit him as long as he kept out of our trenches. He was, oddly, quite polite. He showed me a silent butler he had carved from a single block of ebony. I complimented his talent and started back.

In the fortnight before the game our team worked endless drills—roadwork, lunges, dribbles, foot, head, toe, heels, knees, insteps. Gichuru walked and I ran up and down the sidelines calling out instruction and encouragement. Elasticity and control were our object; our method, a combination of screams, telepathy, and rhetoric. I chalked crosses and circles, arrows and boxes on the board, spinning around my own foggy ideal of teamwork while Gichuru worked on individual essence, trying to infuse a rubbery wisdom into their bodies—a heightened irritability of the limbs that would move the ball with more speed and complexity than Mac's boys could handle.

It was difficult to know it if was working. They only played each other. And their highest accomplishments often seemed to be to please us, their teachers. They hadn't enough of the killer egoism we both thought they needed. We were scared.

In the midst of our apprehension Gichuru was taking

precautions. Next to the name of Mugambi, the watch-man, in the school accounts there was an entry of twenty shillings over and above the normal Land Rover rental fee. "For special assistance at the game." In the mornings when I called Mugambi to help drive away the cows who were eating my vegetables, he'd giggle fu-riously, swat the bovine rumps, and give me a whole praise-song on the wisdom and foresight of Gichuru.

Mugambi has been through a lot. He fought for independence with the Land Freedom Army. Or, as the British say, he was a Mau-Mau. In the days of the Emergency the British came through by day to round up traitors, or at least potential soldiers, and at night the rebels came out of the forest for their own recruit-ing. Mugambi was whipped with the broad side of a panga often enough by both sides that he took to spending a good deal of time up a tree in the woods munching bananas that his daughter brought him. One night the guerrilla band that he had arbored himself to avoid caught the glint of his knife in the starlight, surrounded his tree, and shook him down. A man of resourcefulness, he explained that he'd come to join up and spent the next eighteen months dodging napalm and developing a terror of unseen footsteps. When he came blinking out of the forest he found that a neighbor had quite legally taken his land. His clans-man Gichuru got him the watchman job and, through the purchase of a rundown Land Rover, he became a diligent hauler of other people's goods. He was going

to help us somehow. Gichuru spoke only of contin-
gencies and prescribed deep knee-bends for the team.

MacIntyre's entrance the day of the game—zebra-
striped youths with starched collars; a painted bus,
dentless, shining; a phalanx of supporters in the sunlight. Ah, the cleanliness of that team, the pure pistoned
effort of their warmups! Smooth kicks to the left, then
at a whistle, to the right, up in long stretches, running
in place. Swirls of hip and elbow that if we'd tried would
have landed us in desperate bruised heaps, they carried
out like a policeman's twirled nightstick—deft and potent. Their preparation was perfect, above our hatred.
We regarded them the way sheep must observe power
mowers; they performed the same tasks we did but their
construction and source of power were beyond us.

We had come to the field piled in the old Land Rover.
It hit the gravel of the research station drive, lurched,
and discarded us onto the field. MacIntyre and his
team kept looking at us as if we'd spilled something
on their laps. They were so neat, colorful, scrubbed.
We were going to play soccer against the Easter Parade.

Our captains flipped for direction. The Chorumbe
boy won and after getting confirmation from Mac at
the sideline (Mac nodding gravely, almost in sleep), he
went with the wind. Muriuki spilled the ball between
the two forward lines, leapt aside, and the game was on.

It was not one-sided. But it was not nearly two-sided.
They were the sea, we were the land, and the tide was

up. They had one boy built like a thug, legs almost as big around as a Cape buffalo's belly and a forehead quite as wide and capable as a Cape's horns. He was slow to start but quick and terrible once in motion. Our players, however brave, when faced with the buffalo boy panting down toward them, shied, swerved, and left the field open. Then he would rumble into position, stare blankly dead on the ball, and send low, hard kicks straight to our goalie's teeth.

This inspired fear, but fortunately was not the best way to score. The kicks were too long. Our goalie would see the ball hurtle grand in his vision, like an astronaut viewing the earth when something has gone horribly wrong, and would jerk his hands up to his face (which was of course just the thing to do), saving us and his nose from certain destruction. Some of the Chorumbe schoolboys shouted "Well done!" at the buffalo boy's kicks. But Mac would stare them quiet and call the big boy back to the side. "Pass, you bloody fool," he'd breathe into the boy's ear and then, as our field rules permitted, sit him down on the bench to cool off. With the team's golden calf on the sideline, Mac's discipline, the fierce teamwork he had drummed into them, took over. Obliqueness was everything, the ball skittering from foot to foot, over, around, and underneath us. Our boys threw themselves at the ball—huge long leaps to block a pass with shoulder or chest that missed and sent them skidding across the turf while the Chorumbe players skipped over the bodies and pushed on downfield.

# Our Big Game

Gichuru and I tried to cheer our team on in Kigeli and English. But every smooth steal and stroke of the Chorumbe team brought a roar from MacIntyre's bus-brought claque, a whistle-blast of confidence. All we could muster were murmurs, faint rumblings like rumors in a tyranny.

Mugambi, though, had none of our despondency. He squatted on the sidelines, laughing and patting his kneecaps. In the last minutes of the half we were down two goals. Mugambi looked up to Gichuru. "You will need me now. This is proper." Gichuru nodded. Both moved downfield to where Muriuki was watching. They huddled with him while I kept yelling vain commands to our players, all of us enmired in Mac's excellence.

Halftime came, and Gichuru and I passed around towels and oranges to our team. On the Chorumbe side of the field Mac snapped his fingers and two team managers went around with plastic-spouted water bottles dosing out some sweet, special liquid while the boys cleaned their cleats. There would be a forty-five minute break with a show by local primary-school children. Muriuki invited us all in for tea. He didn't like the taste of coffee.

"You are an artisan these days, Mr. MacIntyre? I have heard of your skill."

A pigtailed girl poured milk and sugar into our cups. "Yes, I like to make things. carving, furniture, scrollwork. It passes the time."

"And you shrink heads?"

Mac's windpipe bubbled.

"Excuse me, isn't this true? I had heard that they were quite wonderful."

"You mean the apples, Mr. Muriuki. I don't shrink heads. I shape them. I work with the fruit. One can carve features into the fruit and then as they dry and wither they begin to take on expressions. Joyful, sad, the whole range. When it achieves just the look you want, you seal it with clear varnish, and it is preserved precisely."

I had seen them in Mac's office. They were horrible. Little grimace-ridden fruitheads. They were the only things he was ever willing to give anybody.

Muriuki persisted. "Have you seen our samba wood? The old Kigeli men made stools from it. Here . . ." He reached to the mantel and drew down a small polished stool about a foot high.

I had never seen one before, at Muriuki's house or anywhere else. It was a smooth round seat on three small graceful legs, each leg carved in the shape of a human figure—a warrior with a spear, a woman carrying a water-gourd, and a tribal elder sitting in judgment. The wood was dark and rich. Like a silk carpet it seemed to change color in different light—now black, now brown, but always above a fire red that leapt out where the wood had been worn smoothest and that underlay the whole.

"With these figures an old man tending cattle would have the whole of the tribe with him. He could sit there comfortably in the sun, his spear on the ground beside him, quiet among the animals of his clan, and content. It is a beautiful thing, isn't it?"

MacIntyre rubbed his palm across the smoothness of the seat. He traced the figures with his fingers. He was about to smile. "It's a fine piece. I've never . . ."

"They are not made anymore. Or not with the same skill."

"This is called 'samba'?" Mac was holding the stool as if it were a bird.

"Yes. The wood's still around though there are only a few groves. One of them is here." Muriuki's grin was as wide as one of the Olympic heroes'. "Five minutes away in the forest. I have a power saw you could use."

"But the game . . ."

We all agreed there was still time. The field was dancing with primary school children singing the national anthem in Swahili and "I'm a Little Teapot" in English.

"Mugambi here knows the path. He can show you the way and you'll be back quickly with your arms full of samba. Consider it a gift of welcome to my house."

Mac still had the stool cupped between his hands. He put it back on the mantel and nodded his head. Muriuki told Mugambi where to get the saw and some rope, and the watchman dashed out the door.

The sun was turned off instantly, like a lamp, when the two of them entered the forest. Mugambi went in front, holding the saw by a thick leather strap. The tool swung by his side in rhythm with his walk, the teeth slimly missing his bare leg with each swing. Mac kept watching it at the instant it swayed nearest the curly hairs on Mugambi's leg. Each time the cutting edges passed clear, the white man freed his gaze. He looked up at the creeper-ridden canopy of the woods, the thick-leaved vines twisting among the evergreens and palms. High at the tops he could see a colobus monkey following them, jumping from tree to tree. Then at a signal from the ticking in Mac's mind, his eyes went down again toward the body of the man in front of him as the teeth of the saw dipped along the bunched muscles of Mugambi's calf, about to cut and draw blood, but always missing.

"I wish you wouldn't do that."

Mugambi stopped and the saw swung out in a semi-circle towards Mac.

"There is no danger here. I know the forest."

"Not the forest, damn it, the saw. Hold it firmly or you're going to slice yourself open."

"Do not mind, sir. These woods are like my home. I fought very near here."

"With the Home Guard?"

Mac had been an officer himself.

"Yes. The Home Guard. They were our enemy. You need not be afraid of the saw, sir, or snakes, leopards, or anything. I will guide you. The place we are going is quite close here."

# Our Big Game

Mugambi was back in full stride. The saw kept swinging and Mac kept watching it, holding his wonder at the forest inside the tick-tock of imagined bloodletting. The path disappeared but Mugambi continued with his neverminds. They ducked under branches and stumbled over fallen logs alive with white slugs and mushrooms big as moons. The watchman, still letting the saw dangle free, paused more often now. Once or twice he backtracked. They were in constant twilight.

Mugambi stopped and blinked very quickly. He brought the fingertips of his free hand to his mouth and looked about in a slow mechanical circle. Everywhere the same dark greens and browns closed over their heads and they were centered in a bubble inside the twining.

"We are lost," he said, crossing his legs to sit down, and then he started yelping in pain.

At the field the primary-school children had sung all their songs. Muriuki, as the official host, decided that the schedule should be followed and the game continued, with or without MacIntyre. The Chorumbe captain's sense of natural authority was confused (as was unavoidable with Mac's students), but he had a solid textbook conception of responsibility. He was a tall, stiff adolescent who moved like a pair of scissors, but had soft, wise eyes that were always near terror. He called a brief huddle, asked his players not to let their courage flag, and reminded them that they were ahead two goals. They clasped hands, cheered, and the game resumed.

But there were no sudden sweeps this time, no Apache charges. The field was clotted, thick, the players slamming into scrums that looked like street-cleaning machines, their upper bodies stuck together and their several feet kicking frantically. There were injuries and outcries, Muriuki running into the clashes to adjudicate. He would blow his whistle, a boy would limp to the sidelines, and a fresh body would dash to the game. Amid the flesh-bumping the buffalo boy began to emerge again. Sometimes he broke out— shaking opponents off and kneeing toward the open field. And sometimes he seemed passive—the boy and ball expelled from the heap, spit out like a bounced drunk and his hat. Once in blue sky and open air, the whole confused crowd of players chasing after him, he leaned forward, gritted his face, every muscle squeezed tight except the dead center, the tip of his nose, and smashed out the same long, mean, pointless kicks as before—which our goalie scooped up or bounced off or headed down until he shook and resounded like an abused bell.

There was no Mac to yank the buffalo boy now. The Chorumbe captain knew what he ought to do. But he was afraid, not of any malevolence on the part of his oak-thighed teammate, but of the buffalo boy's fierce crazy oblivion to anything other than shattering worlds with his foot. Mac might handle that, but nobody sixteen years old and forty pounds lighter could.

So our team started playing to the big man, waiting for the sure turnover. Then they would kick the ball among themselves, juggling it like one of the hearth coals they used to carry as children, each boy more surprised than the last at the possibility of a score, until they sent it on to the Chorumbe goalie—who in the first half could have been comatose. He strained and scrapped at the ball but one, two—now the tie—and three times let it dribble past him.

And so we won. Though the Chorumbe captain called vainly for timeouts and Mac's team in their starch and stripes kept looking to the forest for succor, no one appeared at the threshold. Strain as they might for the flash of his eyes, the shine of his head, there was nothing to see, a deep black hole.

Until the game was over. Muriuki, who during the play had waved away the anxiety of the Chorumbe schoolboys, praising Mugambi's knowledge of the woods, finally relented and called a station worker to send after Mac and our watchman.

But there was no need. The blackness at the edge of the forest suddenly filled and there was Mac, naked to the waist. Cradled under his left arm was a log of dark samba that must have weighed a hundred pounds. Over his right shoulder he pulled a length of rope, the end of which dragged Mugambi riding on a lashed mass of branches and twigs. The watchman was rubbing his ankle with one hand and holding the saw steady with the other. He was singing something very low and growly with an infinity of syllables.

"The man's an absolute fool," Mac said. "But I've taken care of him nonetheless. He at least had the good sense to sprain his ankle not ten feet from the samba trees. As you see, I found the wood on my own, strapped his foot, jerrybuilt this sledge, and found our way out. Quite good, I think, like the dogs pull among the Eskimo or your Western Indians with their ponies."

Mac's team did not greet him. They huddled close around their captain.

"I trust the game has not been unduly delayed?"

Mac dropped the pullrope to Mugambi's sledge, keeping the samba log under his arm, and began to move toward us. Suddenly the Chorumbe captain ran to him out of the circle and began to explain, shoulders back, arms at his side—a terrified classroom declamation. Mac dropped the log.

Gichuru came to him smiling. Madly, he started shaking Mac's hand over and over as if electricity were gluing them together. He was congratulating Mac on his team's play. Mac's white skin went even paler— into a clear glaze that seemed to show the swing and pulse of blood underneath, the striping of the tensed muscles—the transparent man and the black man still shaking hands.

"You are responsible for this," Mac said.

"The decision to resume play was made by the host official. Those are the rules."

Muriuki nodded.

"Then you're both responsible."

"We did what was proper. I am not ashamed."

Mugambi meanwhile was inching himself off the sledge. He raised himself to his feet, leaned in both directions, then made a small circle. Satisfied with his progress he tried some tentative jumps, both feet together, and then like a crazy sunflower burst into ecstatic hopping. "I am fine now," he said, bouncing past the disputation, "I am better. This is better," and pogo-sticked over to the Land Rover already stuffed with our team.

MacIntyre spoke in a soft dead voice. "You are an insult to me, Gichuru. I was your teacher." He wrenched free of the handshake and raised his huge hand up in the air.

Gichuru did not move at all. He spoke from his handsome mask. "Do not strike me, Mr. MacIntyre. I know that you are a hard man." Mac dropped his hand. The two of them backed away from each other, both retreating as one would from a king.

Some of our boys in the Land Rover began to whistle, but Gichuru cut them off and stood quiet. MacIntyre called his schoolboys together and told them to gather their things. The captain with the wise eyes attended Mac, tilting toward him to catch his wishes. He stumbled as he tried to keep up with MacIntyre's long strides toward the bright bus. When the Chorumbe team had gone, Gichuru let the boys hoot and whistle all they wanted. Mac left the log of samba wood on the field.

Since the game Muriuki has returned to his science and coffee beans while Gichuru and I are busy preparing our students for the national examinations. Gichuru is more animated than ever before and shows signs of ambition. He speaks of becoming a politician someday, although on what side of the issues he does not yet know. We still haven't heard from Mac, although I've spoken with Sally. She is worried that he will take the whole business out on his own students—some sort of reign of terror. She says the only lesson he seems to have learned is that there is danger in pity. As for Mugambi, he stays at the old job, running Gichuru's errands and keeping watch at night. He bought a goat with the extra money he earned. It is a large fat creature, and someday soon it will make a feast for us all.

# New England, 1991

## The Sauna After Ted's Funeral

In the sauna after the burial service, Alden dipped into the wrong barrel and poured scalding water on his foot. "*Gesummaria*," said Squillace, a pile of boulders sagging down the wooden bench, "that'll screw you every time." He shook his head in despair. Willi muttered something in Finnish and drained a bucket from the cold tub over Alden's leg. "Now keep it in the water," he commanded. Obedient, Alden thrust his right foot into one of the cold pails and slid his buttocks around to the lower bench. He wriggled his toes. His foot glowed.

Nutbrown, freshly stripped, walked in from the changing room. He bowed his head and marched silently to the top bench. There, with great formality, like a justice about to pronounce sentence of death, he dipped a washcloth in the cold water and placed the square on his head. The terrycloth's front corner dripped a rivulet of cool down his forehead to the tip of his nose. On the sauna's upper and lower benches, the four naked mourners sat themselves in two pairs, bellies looming through the mist.

"You know," said Willi, "together we're more than three hundred years old."

"Just the four of us?"

"Well, maybe two-fifty." He leaned forward and ladled a copper dipper of water onto the layer of rocks that lined the top of the wood stove. A cloud of steam rose. Slowing their breath to avoid the new moisture's burn, stopping movement, the others calculated out Willi's comment. They observed the flaccid muscles of their calves, their piebald reddening skin. The men on top stared at the skulls of the two on the bench below. The tips of their ears burned, and the skin of their napes where the points of hot, wet hair brushed. In the once cold pail, Alden's foot stopped throbbing as the water heated to a soothing lukewarm.

"When I was younger, in Mexico," he said, the heat and cold reminding him, "I loved to swim. I was working for United Shoe in Leon, building a factory. They were using those damn bamboo scaffolds. We would lose a man every week because no one knew what they were doing. Falls and sheer stupidity. Once I saw two workers with paint buckets just trying to be polite. The one leaned out too far, making this Alphonse-and-Gaston gesture, and his bucket caught on a pole and he went right over, blue paint with him. His ribs were broken and they punctured his lung." Alden paused. The air in the wooden cabin was too hot for speaking. He closed his eyes, then began again more softly, more slowly. "The guy who sent us the workers had connections with the CTM, the government union. He was always trying to get me to meet his sister."

"Oh, come on."

"I'm serious. I'm not talking about Tijuana. This was a sad story. She was a widow with a kid. They wouldn't talk about the husband. She was one of the most beautiful women I have ever seen. Gray eyes, a coppery-brown cast to her hair, fair skin. And beautiful arms"—for some seconds, Alden thought—"like a diver's."

"Dark and exotic?" said Squillace, suspicious.

"No, I don't mean that. She didn't look . . ."

"Mexican?"

"No, she didn't. A lot of Mexicans don't. She looked like an American woman. But I had never really spoken with her. She and her little boy would just come with the brother to the site office sometimes. The brother was a real hustler but he liked to give the impression that he was in a leisure class, that his work was just an extension of his family life. Actually, Alma—the sister—was going to a secretarial school, and I had a sense that their financial situation was pretty precarious. But if you'd asked him what his profession was, I think he would have laughed and said he was a labor contractor and a part-time chaperone. They had drawing-room manners which went completely over my head, but he didn't know that."

Alden took a new breath of the heavy air and rubbed his hands over his chest. He dug a thumb into the sore muscles just below his collar bone and felt a whisper of heartache. The loosening of flesh with its intimation of mortality disturbed him. Relaxation was not necessarily a friend. He was beginning to fear that the weekly sessions in the moist heat were becoming irrevocable.

Next to him, Squillace moved a loofah in circles over the old skin of his knees. "So the brother wanted you to marry this woman?"

"He was interested. There were five of us from the company and I was the only bachelor. And he knew I was an engineer. That's a bigger deal in Latin countries; it's a certificate, a title like duke or doctor. But I think he really liked me. I don't think he appreciated how genuinely ordinary I was."

"They worship Americans," pronounced Nutbrown from above, his eyes closed in bliss.

"No. They worship money like everybody else. He was a man who made a living off the people he knew and, down there, Americans are always good to know. I enjoyed the respect. Anyway, he invited me to a picnic with Alma and the boy, on a Sunday afternoon. There was a small lake outside the city, behind an earthen dam, a *presa*, that had only been built the year before. The hills around were maguey fields, the plant they make tequila from, and rope, too, at that time. Big plants with rings of thick green leaves. They look like giant artichokes, as big as a man, and from the center, at the right time of year, grow these trunks seven or eight feet high with branches emerging at perfect right angles. We used to call them toothbrush trees, but they're really immense reproductive stalks, coated with bristles."

Nutbrown, the eldest, opened his eyes. "It sounds terrifying."

"It's not. If you assume you're on a different planet, it's perfectly normal. It's just unreal. Between the plants there wasn't a living thing growing, not a weed, just brown dirt. The lake lay at the bottom of the hills and in its center was an island, a smaller hill drowned when the dam was built. It was gentle and green and at the highest point there was a statue of Father Hidalgo—he's their Thomas Jefferson—with a torch raised in his hand. Fishermen would row you back and forth from the road by the dam.

"Though the sun was burning on the day we went, it had been raining for some weeks before. The water was silty and abnormally high. The river that fed the lake came straight down from the Sierra and its water was cold and seemed even more so in the new heat. We had to wear sweaters as we rowed over to the island, then, almost as soon as we set foot on the grass, we had to take them off."

Squillace lumbered down the two short steps from his seat on the lower bench. In automatic movements, he submerged a bucket in the cistern of cold water, held it still, then lifted it brimming and emptied it over the top of his head. He dropped the bucket to the concrete floor and passed a thick hand around the shape of his skull. He shook his head briskly, scattering drops, and began to massage shampoo into the curled remnants of his youthful hair. As Squillace rubbed, an animal noise grew from his mouth, halfway between a sigh and a death-groan. Water, from the first bucketful of a minute before, dripped over his skin as over the terraces of an ornate fountain, pooling in the folds of his flesh.

Nutbrown, a man of normal weight, stared in horror. "You're a wonder, Bobby. Aren't you ever going to lose a couple of pounds?"

Squillace chuckled from underneath his cap of foam.

"Not in your lifetime."

"Or yours maybe," said Nutbrown, not pleased at the implication.

"Don't give me grief." The younger and heavier man glared upward, then sat down on the steps and bent over, hiding his face as his fingers pressed soap into the fur behind his ears. "Whose shampoo is this anyway?" he said, nursing his wound. "It's gummy."

On high, Nutbrown grinned. "Don't blame me, Bobby. That was Ted's."

Alden resumed his story. "The sister and I didn't really have much to say to each other. My Spanish was all right then, but it was as if she wasn't actually there to talk. She was there to have attentions paid to her, of a certain Mexican kind, and I didn't know how to manage that. So I played with the boy and tried to talk business with the brother. But I could see that they were misinterpreting my inadequacy. If I was tongue-tied and awkward, it was because I was circumspect and deep. If I felt compelled to talk about work—pointless speculations about the next day's problems—it was not because I was ill at ease and desperate, but because I was businesslike and matter-of-fact.

"Then she asked me about the Abominable Snowman. It was not an uncommon question. It was always in the *Reader's Digest* then, both in English and Spanish. There was something about it that captured their interest in Americans and snow and monsters from the North. And Alma—I think I see now—was also trying to help me, to come up with this safe, ridiculous topic to talk about. So I told them what I thought, that I had never seen one, but that they could exist in places where people seldom went. Not a man really, but a creature very like a man, upright and active, and living by himself. And while I was looking at the food set out on the tablecloth—there was a cold fish salad, I remember, and tamales that they had kept warm in napkins over the boat ride—being hungry and spouting this nonsense about the Snowman, I noticed the water rushing by. Behind the grass and the few little trees, the water of the lake was sliding away."

Squillace lifted his face to Alden, his wide hand on his forehead keeping the soap from his eyes. "There's no current in a lake."

"There was in this, a slight one. They had two small wooden sluices on either side of the earth-dam, where the water turned mills, but this was different. It was as if we were in a boat or as if the lake had become a river again. It was pouring by. There was white foam and the beginning of long waves. Behind it all was a groan, a rumble of thunder that didn't stop. It was like the tearing of an endless, strong cloth right beside your ear."

Willi drew the copper ladle from the bucket where bundles of birch twigs soaked and flung water on the heated stones. Again the wooden cabin filled with stinging mist. "That's good, Willi," said Nutbrown. The washcloth now rested on his uptilted features, a small shroud. "That hits the spot." Each word fluttered the terrycloth.

Squillace turned his face to Alden. "So what was it?"

"The *presa*. It had soaked through underneath and rotted with the rain. From our island we could see where it had broken, where the water rushed, and the men dancing on the edges of the gap. But what was a torrent by us, a whirl of water, seemed slowed down at the dam. Workers appeared from nowhere, as if a truck had just suddenly come by and dropped them off. It was always like that in Mexico. People without work were always moving around at the edge of your vision waiting for a catastrophe. That was how the brother made a living: sending signals to those people. But they didn't have a clue what to do. They ran across the top to the damage, then backed away. They tried to open the sluices wider to ease the pressure, but then they must have closed them for a time because at one point the water seemed to back up. There was a reverse wave, a straight line of muddy foam that moved over the top of the downward flow, back from the dam up toward the mountains. The water was sloshing around this drowned valley as if it were a giant bathtub and someone was monkeying with the drain."

Nutbrown slid the cloth off his eyes. "Were you safe?" he asked.

"I don't know. It was hard to think about. If the valley was just draining, in spite of all the wildness of the water, then the safest thing would have been to climb to the center of the island—the center of a hill it really was—and stay by the statue. The real danger was downstream of the dam. But it was hard to concentrate one's mind on what was going on. There was an attraction to the water, the way people go down to the beach in a storm. The dam break had turned the water alive. We were watching a creature."

On sudden inspiration, Willi reached out to lift one of the tied bundles of twigs from the bucket by his feet. The pail handle jumped, clattering at the touch. "Don't worry, Alden," he said. "I'm still listening." Methodically, Willi began to whisk his calves with the fragrant leaves.

"We were standing frozen, the mother, the uncle, and I, looking out toward the dam, while the boy stared at the edge of the water and the land. He was mesmerized. You have to understand this whole island was just a lawn. There was the picnic blanket, a few trees, and then a storm, as if a standard-issue suburban house and yard had been thrown into the sea. There was no sand, no border, nothing to warn him away. He inched down the grass toward the edge, his eyes fixed on the rush of water. The flow was carrying earth and branches. Stunned fish floated on the top. There were frogs and snakes, all moving by us. The boy knelt to put his hand in and lost his balance on the muddied grass. He slipped into the water and Alma screamed, a long, siren scream that flowed into the thunder of the rushing water and the breaking dam. The brother grabbed his walking stick, ran down the few feet of lawn, and leapt in after the boy."

"That was stupid," said Squillace.

"Yeah, it was. But it was a very Mexican thing to do. I think I understood it." Alden leaned his head back against the moist boards and slumped down into the hot, damp breeze that pushed from the stove. He raised his eyes. Outside, through the small window that clung under the eaves, it had started to snow.

"What did you do?"

"I tried to get the boy. I ran down the island toward the dam. There was a small tree at that end, hardly more than a bush really, near the edge. I wrapped my legs around the roots and leaned the lowest branches out over the water. The boy was coming fast, five or ten yards behind me. I yelled at him to take hold, but with the noise and his fear, I'm sure he couldn't hear me. The yelling was for me, to convince me I was doing something. I pushed down on the branch just as he drew near. I heard his head smash into the wood and then the current spun him around lengthwise against the branches and started to slide him away from me. I reached in the water—it was freezing cold and, above all the swarming mud, the topmost layer where the boy was floating seemed fresh from the mountains, clear and green—and yanked. All I could hold was the boy's hair. He had long , flowing, Indian hair, slippery in my hand, but it was enough. I rolled off the tangle of branches that had propped me up and pulled him from the water."

"You were a hero."

"Yeah. I'd nearly opened his skull with the branch. There was blood all down the side of his face, but he was alive."

"I'm serious," said Squillace, soaking the shampoo from his hands in a cookpot of cold water. "You saved his life."

Nutbrown put his hands on the rail and leaned from the top bench. "And the brother? Did he die?"

"No, he didn't. He was badly hurt, but he didn't die. He was thrown against one of the mill sluices and they pulled him out there with his back broken. I visited him later at the hospital and he told me how extremely grateful to me he was for saving his nephew. He kept mentioning the tree; it was as if he were saying, 'Why didn't I think of that?' But at the time, on the island, when he'd jumped, we couldn't see anything. We just saw him go. I wrapped my shirt around the boy's head while his mother held him, and we waited.

"Within a half hour the lake emptied. The old valley came back, revealed and destroyed at the same time. At the very bottom, below the maguey fields and the toothbrush trees, below the walls of mudslide and debris, the river lost itself in what must have been its path before the dam, a ravine choked with trees and earth. There were colors everywhere, picked out by the sun. The brown dirt from the maguey field bled red streaks down into the lake bed and there were rock outcrops washed white where they were too steep to catch the mud. Scattered about, at five or six spots, were bodies, their clothes washed clean by the flood. At that distance, in the strong light and the glare from the wetness, the faces and the feet disappeared. All you could see were their clothes, dots of color as if they were something inside the eye, the clothes of drowned men. The sun was so bright."

Alden bent his head over and shook it slowly in the comforting steam. He closed his eyes. "We waited several more hours, leaning against the statue of Hidalgo, hoping that we could be seen. The boy needed to be carried and I couldn't see the two of us navigating the mud and managing the boy at the same time. The picnic food was still waiting on the tablecloth set on the grass. We gave the boy some water and tried to talk, but we couldn't really. Alma thanked me for my help in florid Spanish, very politely and very formally, and held her son's head in her lap as he slept. I was just as embarrassed, just as ignorant of what to say as I had been before the catastrophe. I had saved her son's life and I still couldn't make conversation. My awkwardness reassured me. It was a comfortable, small worry in the face of destruction.

"But I could still see the valley around me: the green maguey plants on dusty hillsides above us, and below, the inside of the earth, mud and rock and tangled trees, the bodies of fishes, and animals, and men. When help finally came to us—they brought with them a bag of boots and medicine and a stretcher for the boy—we walked out through the valley. Even as we walked the mud was drying. The sun burnt it from on top and underneath, the desert land drew down the moisture. A year's drowning had softened the shape of the land and piled earth in strange, deceptive places. But what struck me was that the land was still organized. There were mounds and shapes: the foundations of lost houses, the worn traces of fields. We walked through ruins, an old world. And I thought that when the lifeblood of something—of the land, of a person—suddenly drains away, that underneath everything is its death, not a flat, meaningless terrain, but a place with organization and shape." Alden opened his eyes and with his fingertips wiped the sweat from his eyebrows.

"So is that what you think? Life is on top of death?" Squillace, puzzled, a bundle of birch twigs unmoving in his hand, peered up at Alden under a damp forehead. Nutbrown, from the hottest, highest seat, looked down. Willi, barely listening, sat silent in his corner and scrubbed dead skin from the soles of his feet with a laundry brush.

"I guess so. What I saw weren't Mayan ruins or cities. Ancient isn't the right word. It was everyday. The remnants of people's lives; the old habitations worn smooth. When I think of the valley of death now, that's what I see. That is what I remember."

Nutbrown exhaled, a thin, trailing sigh. Then he gulped in awe. "Jesus Christ, it's snowing!"

Alden bridled. "I thought I told you that."

"No you didn't." The older man turned his face, annoyed.

Willi laid down his brush and, in equanimity toward his friends, spoke to the stove. "Had enough heat?"

"For a while," muttered Nutbrown. He eased himself off the upper bench with stiff arms and descended the short steps to the cement floor. Squillace drew up his bulk and fell in behind him toward the door. Willi and Alden awaited their turns in the narrow room, a parade of old, naked men.

They stepped out into the changing room at the front of the cabin. Squillace drew a towel from a pile and, wrapping it with difficulty around his waist, he sat in the quiet cool. In a line around the walls, hung from wrought iron hooks, the sauna-goers' funeral suits and respectful ties sprawled with their boxer shorts and the torn ribbing of old and favored undershirts. A whistle of wind coursed under the metal of the roof.

Squillace shifted. He rubbed the white hairs of his chest. "So did you marry the sister?"

Alden cocked his head and stared him down. "You know I didn't. I came back here and married your sister."

"Just curious." Squillace lowered the folds of his chin down to his breastbone and smiled.

"You gutless wonders!" harrumphed Nutbrown. He stood and threw open the front door.

The wind snapped it wide. Outside a storm was growing. The snow fell over Willi's back lawn, the flowerbeds, the ghost-shapes of rocks, out to the gray pond and the late autumn woods beyond. Nutbrown padded out into the twilight blow, his lined skin shining copper in the purified light from the changing room's bulb. He whirled a couple of steps, his vulnerable body braced in the wash of snow, the soles of his feet about to freeze fast. "It's grand," he said, "from the ankles up." In the sudden atmosphere of winter, the sauna steam rose from Nutbrown in billows. It poured off his chest and swirled from his arms to mingle with the cloud of his speech. He hopped again, his feet in snowy pain. The steam danced about his head and shoulders, a warm, wet halo in the cabin's light, until he looked, to the younger men staring out the door, for all the world like an aged angel consumed in God's moist fire.

# Kenya, 1971

## Mobley's Troubles

Mobley kicked the box a couple of times, made a kind of barking noise, then waited a few seconds before picking it up. He was terribly afraid of snakes. You could stumble across them anywhere, like tripping over your own clothes in a morning bedroom. A boy down the road from the mission station had run over a black mamba with his bicycle during the short rains, a few months before. The animal bit and the fangs grazed the child's heel, piercing the skin before the snake's body was twisted in the spokes. The boy died within fifteen minutes, fallen over the bike at the side of the road, the dead snake caught in the wheel.

So Mobley would give them warning and time to go away. Because of the heat he was packing in the yard while Martha walked up and down the doorpath into the house, carrying out their possessions one or two at a time. She piled them on the newly mown lawn beside him—Bibles and prayerbooks, a thin twisty cane blacked with shoe polish to look like ebony that a Kigeli elder had given him, old suits and dresses with

47

moth flakes in the pockets, a boy's baseball bat, a couple of toolboxes. A furry hyrax which he'd shot and stuffed stood on the walk getting wet in the sprinkler, marbles for eyes.

The old frame house had been built by the founders. Surrounded by the paved sidewalk and the bluegrass lawn, it looked more American than African, except for the sprinkler which whirled its water erratically, too slow, too fast, echoing the pulses sent from the ram pump down at the waterfall behind the house.

Jody Ross came up from the school building to help in the packing. Ross was a Scotsman under government contract to teach science at the secondary school. Except for the Mobleys he avoided the missionaries and spent his spare time stringing together the past of the Kigeli from the tales the old men told him over gourds of sugar beer. At night he'd get quietly drunk on his own whiskey, poring over the maps he'd drawn of the path the tribe took when they climbed into the highlands from the northern desert. Jody was a good listener and unlike the missionary men he could handle long silences. Mobley was fond of long silences. Jody and he got along.

The old couple and the Scotsman made a few more trips into the house, then Martha brought out iced tea, and they sat down on folding chairs while Mobley cut off lengths of Indian twine to wrap the boxes.

"This is a beautiful place," he said. Dropping the rope and knife on his lap, he looked out over the blue hills to Lake Victoria, a bright gash of silver at the sky's edge. The sky itself was brilliant, royal—white dancing clouds everywhere.

Ross asked him if he'd stay if he had the choice. He said he would.

Of course he didn't have the choice. The Inland Mission Board was sending him home, nominally because the Mobleys had already been in Africa three years beyond the twenty the Board prescribed for their lay missionaries. But that rule had been winked in the past. The truth was they thought he had become too cranky and old for the job. And the constant taxidermy disturbed the Board. Mobley was dwindling off into privacy, and the missionaries no longer trusted him.

The common wisdom was that Bob's troubles had cracked him. Bob was Kigeli, an orphan whose parents had died of cholera when he was ten. He had relatives who had room and food for him but no money to send him to school. To pay his way he began to do odd jobs around the mission station, sweeping the bright red cement floors, saving the bottles that the missionaries were often inclined to throw away. Bob wore glasses. None of the other school children had them. They were large flat spectacles in a black metal rim that gave him a clerical, trustworthy appearance. The mission Americans all liked him and touted his talents back and forth to each other, even though he'd been raised as a Catholic.

That wasn't a serious matter. His older sister had

been in a Catholic primary school at the time of his birth, so they had a father baptize him. The local African priest worked off an alphabetical list of Christian names, which he gave out in order. Bob's real name was Balthazar.

Hank Mobley had a distrust of that kind of Biblical name as somehow un-Christian, so he started calling the boy Bob. The two loved each other at once. Hank gave Bob a black elastic band to keep his glasses on, and for the first time in his life the boy could play soccer without the fear that the principal financial investment of his extended family would slip down his nose and shatter. Hank also sent away back home and bought Bob a bat, a mitt, and a ball. They'd go out into the fallow fields and knock grounders and flies to each other, chasing the ones they missed off into the banana groves. In the mission's forty years Bob was the first African they let know about baseball.

Bob spent his nights at home, but he walked in every morning, mud or dust, for work, and on Sunday he went to church with the Mobleys. He was the only young African there although there were a few older people—women in green dresses and men in World War II British Army raincoats.

Both the men and the women were old enough to have long drooping earlobes which had been pierced and stretched when they were children to hold large ornamental plugs. Now they no longer wore the jewelry and some of the women folded the lobes up over the tops of their ears for neatness' sake. The Mission Church didn't represent all of Protestant Christendom in Kigeli. The largest group of Christians—fervent, devout, and distressingly puritanical—had broken off from the Americans and started a church with their own preachers on a lone hill behind the main market in town. They still helped support the Kigeli Mission hospital and school, but they preferred their own spiritual direction, setting the hymn texts to Kigeli melodies and accompanying the songs on goatskin drums rather than the mission's tubercular organ.

But Reverend McCall, the minister at the American chapel, still preached as if the white stone hall was full of untutored heathen rather than the families of earnest medical missionaries who actually sat before him. His face was wrinkled, his body stooped and savaged by time. Nothing of his youth was left but the thick head of Arthur Godfrey red hair that bushed off his scalp. His sermons were insane parables in a 400-word vocabulary plucked from Longman's Simplified English about how the Kingdom of God is a hut that never leaks. They were filled with Aesopian animals from every possible continent—lions, monkeys, kangaroos, raccoons—leading strange cautionary lives that at the end of the story always sucked them into the whirlpool of salvation. Most of the time he was completely unintelligible. During the week he subsided to a quiet life saying graces and leading the moments of joint doctor–patient prayer that were required before operations at the hospital.

When the service was over, Bob went to the Mobleys' for Sunday dinner. After a week of corn, beans, and millet cakes, on the Sabbath Bob gorged on meat. In the eyes of the Kigeli, the missionary homes were built on meat, their basement freezers filled with the cold carcasses of pigs and cattle. It wasn't that the Kigeli minded the killing. They wrung the necks of chickens and roasted goats for feasts. But the scale of the Americans' slaughter amazed the people—bacon in the morning, mutton for lunch, a roast for dinner, all the fine fat platters dripping scraps for the cats and dogs. Bob respected the linen napkins and the translucent china, the smooth strong curves of the Mobleys' walnut table, but nothing held for him such wonder as the plates full of flesh. He got to like ham and pork, which he'd never before eaten. "Have another slice," Martha would beam, the pink slab wedged between the bright knife and fork. "Go on, it's good for you."

Bob always had the extra slice, and the potatoes with fresh butter, the beans from the Mobley garden that they ate pods and all, the dark sweet iced tea without milk. After the meal they would set the chairs out on the lawn. Hank would take off his shirt and dangle his head over the back of the chair in the sun while Martha read out a Bible lesson. When she finished she'd put the pressed rose she used as a marker back between the pages and snap the book shut. Hank would straighten and call Bob over to him, dress him right up face to face, and look hard in his eyes. "Now you remember every word, son, every word." The sunlight poured around their faces, glinting in Hank's white hair and brows, doubling itself on the big flat circles of Bob's glasses. Bob, his stomach full, lazy in the heat, knew this was supposed to be an important moment, that Hank was trying very hard to mean something. Every Sunday he answered the same, what Hank wanted, his mind full of "Yes, sir," and confusion.

Then he would help Hank go on his rounds. Hank was the missionary for the machines. He took care of the mission's vital organs, the pumps that fed the faucets, the big electrical generators. There were two generators, one for the hospital that ran continuously and one for the missionary homes. The home generator ran only at night, part of its energy recharging the giant battery packs that kept the lamps, freezers, washers, and dryers going through the day and that nestled against the porches and sides of the identical houses like huge hearing aids. Hank also maintained the hospital apparatus—the sterilizers, x-ray machines, and oscilloscopes. His gift was uncanny, God-given. He could fix anything. In the operating room he would kneel by a wounded respirator, poke around for a minute, his eyes tight and intent. Then he'd pull back as though it were a '52 Ford and he a Tennessee mechanic sliding out from underneath on his trolley. "That's it," he'd grin, "over there." He'd pluck out the tube, solder the wires, and the thing would purr. The nurses and doctors, the patients padding by in their long gowns, all would stand amazed. None of them had any entrance to the mystery of Hank's talent. None could pierce its perfection.

Bob tagged behind carrying the two toolboxes, one filled with tubes, plugs, and wire, the other heaped with wrenches, springs, and bolts. He caught the sparks of glory that trailed Hank as he tended his mechanical garden. Bob wasn't quite an apprentice, though. No one could be. Hank was something of an idiot savant. He couldn't explain what he was doing. When he tried, little flashes of intuition bounced about with no discernible connection like loose bolts in a hubcap. He would try to tell Bob how a burning wick in a kerosene refrigerator could make things cold, but it never made sense. So Bob, who was always clever at school with neat handwriting, accurate sums, and a gift for English, never really understood how Hank's mind worked to do the things of which the man was most proud.

Sunday evenings in the short twilight, Hank and he would toss the baseball back and forth on the lawn while Martha stood watching. The couple was getting old, Martha's pear-shaped body falling down in a slow mortal sag while Hank's, once that of a big, muscular man, still fought to maintain its uplift though it pudged at the center, spilling over his stomach and unguarded flanks. But it wasn't the age that separated Bob from them so much as the screens that hid the workings of their minds. Inside the old man was a wizard who could make the material world dance, and behind Martha's

eyes lay some beautiful Baptist garden where bright
birds sang of prophecy and discipline in voices that
she could never translate. Bob tossed the baseball out
and back, again and again, like a spider shooting out its
threads to catch hold of something. And Hank tossed
the ball right back. They never made the connection.

When Bob was fourteen and starting secondary
school, Hank arranged to get him a job in the market
with V.S. Patel, the hardware and sundries dealer who
was the school's principal outfitter. Bob could use the
money to help the Mobleys pay his school fees. Patel,
an Indian, was not keen on the idea of having an African schoolboy working for him. But he agreed to the
idea to placate the missionaries, his most substantial
customers.

Patel was an extremely fat man with excited tiny
features that rolled around his face like peas on a plate.
But his fat was deceptive, like a weightlifter's or a Japanese wrestler's—there was strength underneath it.
The missionaries considered him a pagan. The Kigeli
thought him an outlander. But for twenty years he
had ridden through their distrust and secured his tin
roof and stone walls and the courtyard full of flowers.
However narrow the frontiers of his vision, he was still
lord of all he surveyed.

Which is why he minded particularly when Bob started stealing from him. Bob had learned a manic generosity from the Mobleys. They had surrounded him with
gifts—sneakers, a raccoon cap, nylon fishing lines, fresh

white shirts. In turn Bob opened his employer's store-room to his classmates. Within a few months the boys all had black belts with "007" buckles, the girls, new ribbons in their hair. Under their beds they kept piles of extra writing supplies—blue Chinese pens and exercise books with "ADVENTURE!" printed across the cover, rays of light shooting off it, and underneath, a small boy and girl holding hands and looking at the shining word. Bob, who kept the inventory and delivered Patel's bills, added the goods he spirited off to the account of the Catholic secondary school at Kimbwa, a few hills over toward the lake. The Kimbwa school clerk was a small, very dark man from one of the western tribes. He had prematurely white hair, always wore a suit and tie, and wrote the school correspondence in an ecstatic Victorian longhand. He started sending letters to Patel, writing across the front of the envelope, "ATTENTION! In re accounting errors! Please refer to chief bookkeeper! Immediately!" Patel was in the habit of rejecting all such claims as scurrilous and let the letters go unanswered until the Kimbwa clerk sent over two priests to Kigeli to address their inquiries personally. Patel hemmed and hawed the fathers until they left, then called over Bob, who was standing behind the counter talking to three school friends who all had identical pink plastic combs sticking out of their back pockets.

There was little Bob could do. The combs were on the list of mysterious items sent to Kimbwa. He confessed and Patel started slapping him in the face. Bob, nearly fully grown, already had the body of a large man, but his instincts were still a child's. He took the blows passively, clutching at his spectacle frames to protect them from the Indian's huge hands. Then he stood by the glass counter shaking while Patel plucked the pink combs out of the schoolboys' shorts and yelled them out of the shop.

It was Kavulu, the new policeman, who told Hank about the arrest. He came from the dry eastern part of the country and frequently got lost in the Kigeli forests. He was a tall man, always very tired, with a long head that often seemed about to fall off to the side. He carried himself delicately, like a juggler trying to balance a plate on a long stick. Still he shared a reputation for cruelty with all the non-Kigeli policemen. As he climbed up the hill to the mission and asked the women digging in their gardens where the Mobleys lived, their answers were cautious and afraid.

"You are Mr. Mobley, the friend of Balthazar Chacha?"

The missionaries did not generally let adult Africans into their homes, and Hank and Kavulu stood on the veranda talking while the cloth of the policeman's baggy blue shorts snapped in the breeze. His English was slow and careful.

"Patel, the merchant, the one who has complained against the boy, he says we should talk with you before going further. You gave him a reference for Chacha, isn't it?"

Hank said that he had.

Kavulu smiled. "Then you have excuses?" But Hank said he had no excuses.

"You know—" the policeman sighed, then grinned. "Thank you, madam."

Martha had come out with cups of hot white tea.

"You know, this is a young, ignorant boy, and this Patel, he is an angry man. The people do not like him much. Even myself, I do not like him. If you went to him, to stop him from the prosecution, it would be good." Hank agreed that it would be a good thing.

Kavulu wanted Hank to go talk to Patel as soon as possible, and the missionary promised he would go into Kigeli the next morning. Then they shook hands.

"This makes me very happy, you know. If this thing went on, the boy would go to jail for a long time, even though he is only a boy. The President has told us to be cruel with thieves. He has said they should all be hanged by the neck until they die. But myself, I think that is too much."

Hank said he thought so, too.

They finished their tea silently. Kavulu put the tea-cup down, stretched, and wiped his lips with a starchy handkerchief. He was just about to leave when Martha came out again, asked him if he read English, and handed him a bunch of mission pamphlets. Everybody thanked everybody, and Kavulu walked on down the path to town until his head teetered out of view.

"Goddamn it," Hank said, about to swear louder but then thinking better of it. All his speech was a constant battle against profanity, a battle led by his wife, who quiet in her armchair knitting could grow terrible at the first breath of an oath. "I don't see how this could have happened, I never. . . ." And he sputtered off. They both shook their heads.

The next day Hank drove into Kigeli in the Land Rover. The police wouldn't let him see Bob until he had talked with Patel, so he went quickly over to the market and the wide shop washed in blue paint. Behind Patel's shop was a lush courtyard lined by a triple row of yellow flowers. In its center was an old, strong avocado tree, twice as tall as the low-ceilinged rooms around the yard. Its lower limbs stretched across the whole space from flowerbed to flowerbed, and its crown vibrated with the dark shapes of weavers and long-tailed widowbirds hopping and stumbling among the leaves and heavy fruit. Tied to the lowest limb by a thin brass chain was a large grey parrot with an old woman's eyes. Patel sat at a small table breaking cashews and feeding them to the bird.

"I am practically alone now, Mr. Mobley, except for my mother, who is old and ill. My children are away. You have not met them, I think?"

"No, I haven't, Mr. Patel. I can't say I have." Mobley sat with his back straight and taut, his old fishing hat crumpled in his lap.

"Then you must see them." Patel got up from his chair, avoided a sleeping cat who mewed in slight irritation, and retrieved two photographs from behind the counter inside the shop. The pictures were elaborately framed in black with wreaths of tiny fresh flowers around them as if they were portraits of the newly dead.

"This is Bimla. She is studying at the university in Dar, political science. She is engaged to a polyglot. The man went to Oxford and can speak nine languages. I don't even know the names of all of them.

"Besides his knowledge," Patel waved his finger, "he is healthy and quite rich." He rested his hands on his thighs, the fingers turned inward. "We are all quite satisfied.

"My boy, Dev, is pursuing studies in your country, Las Vegas." The photograph on the table was of two dark, blurred men wearing tee shirts and leaning against the wing struts of a Piper Cub with "The Rennie Landers School of Aviation" painted on the fuselage.

"He will be a pilot. There are many opportunities these days for pilots. But you know," Patel leaned over toward Hank, "such studies are expensive, very expensive." He shook his head and laughed a coughy laugh which the grey parrot picked up and softly echoed.

"I've come to talk about Bob, about Balthazar . . . ," Hank started, then stopped. When he talked he was always either silent or direct. He knew it cut down his room for maneuver, but he could never manage subtlety. "The police said you wanted to talk with me before continuing the case. I thought maybe if I could repay, if . . ."

"You know, sir, this is a serious matter." Patel stood

up and began to circle around the table with his hands clasped behind his back, sliding against the white silk of his kurta. "This is a prison matter. These were not trifles. The goods themselves, 1500 shillings, perhaps more. How can I tell? The boy himself, you know, kept the accounts. You see I trusted him very much, on your say-so, Mr. Mobley, on your say-so."

Patel stood behind Hank's back, declaiming over his head toward the parrot and the tree. "Well then, 1500 for the goods plus the cost of reordering, the petrol, the deliveries, the loss of future accounts from Kimbwa." Patel moved back around the table and sat down again.

"And my own aggravation and suffering, Mr. Mobley, my own suffering. These are not easy things to repay. These are not easy things at all." He slumped his head forward on his hands. Hank was surprised at the fervor. He thought Patel might cry and he wouldn't know what to do. His fingers ached for a tool.

They sat there for some minutes, the two men with their broad shoulders and large heads—Patel's hair black, thick, and straight; Hank's, white and shaggy—staring around each other across the little table while the widowbirds chirruped in the tree.

Then Patel's mother wandered into the courtyard mumbling a torrent of Gujerati, her head wreathed in smoke. She carried an old Lyle's Golden Syrup can in her hands with holes punched in the top to form a shallow brazier. In the pan were lumps of hashish, glowing faintly and sending billows of thick white smoke up to swirl around her smiling face and cling in her hair. The smoke was extravagant, solid, puffing everywhere like an orange-grove smudge pot. She seemed quite happy in her private atmosphere and nodded greetings to Hank and her son.

Patel was outraged. He hissed a bunch of Aryan aspirates at her through his teeth. The mother looked offended, whirled around with her sari like a drunken matador, and returned to the small room from which she had emerged. Patel's glare lingered after her a few seconds, then he took a clean handkerchief out of his pants pocket and wiped his brow.

"Stomach powders, you know. She is ill and takes these stomach powders from India. Very . . ." His English had been fluffed by the return to Gujerati and his own embarrassment. He dangled for a second. "Very . . . hygienic."

The bargaining silence returned. Hank fidgeted.

"What if I gave you 2500 shillings and promised the police that I'd look out for the boy, that I'd be responsible for him? Would you drop the charges? They won't go ahead without your help."

"Twenty-five hundred shillings?"

"I could write a check now. The money is in my account."

"I think I will do this, Mr. Mobley. I think it is fair. I . . ." Patel stopped again and looked at the portraits of his children. He was almost apologetic. "I think you will give me dollars, though. I will need dollars. The boy's studies are very expensive. Learning to fly, it takes time and money. The dollars would help me most."

"Sure. I'll give you dollars. That's fine."

"Cash dollars?"

"Yes, cash dollars." Hank wanted only to get out and get back home now. He started walking out through the shop past the barrels of nails and clasps, the piles of large, broad-blade pangas smeared with packing grease and not yet sharpened, the plastic tumblers full of ball-point pens. "Tomorrow, I'll be back here tomorrow. It'll all be OK." At the doorway Hank stumbled into the cat, who screeched loudly at him. Patel laughed and called out from the courtyard not to mind. As Hank stepped into the Land Rover the parrot picked up the sounds, chuckling and mewing to itself in the avocado tree while the missionary gunned the engine.

The drive home up to the hills was hell. A shower turned the road to mud. The four-wheel drive gears kept slipping out, and Hank was blind with rage against blackmail and injustice, incompetence, and all forms of human weakness.

He stepped to the front door coated with red mud, and Martha made him wash himself off with the hose before she let him in. After he had showered and put on fresh clothes, they took out the cash together and counted it into an envelope for Patel.

The next day he delivered the money and got Bob out of jail. Back at the mission they lectured the boy, and his activities were limited to cutting the missionary lawns with Hank's power mower. He agreed to give Hank and Martha half his earnings until he'd paid back at least a good part of the 1500 shillings Hank told him he'd given the merchant. Bob took his punishment quietly, working hard, but spending more time off the compound and less at the Mobleys, though he still came to Sunday dinner. Hank and Martha thought he might be growing up or away, but they didn't know how to tell.

Two months after the arrest, at the height of the rains, came what Beulah Whittaker took to calling the night of the long knives. Beulah, from New Orleans, was the newest doctor at the mission, but she was not a missionary nor even a teetotaler. She didn't believe in the pre-operation prayers of Reverend McCall, though silent behind her surgical mask she would defer to them, bowing her head and tapping her gloved fingers, almost on the table but still in the air, so as not to contaminate them. Then she would send McCall out of the room and get to work.

Hank admired her matter-of-factness and, when he began to have trouble sleeping, went to her for help. She gave him some mild barbiturates which he sometimes took too many of. On the night of the long knives, the storm, beating on the corrugated tin of the roof, had been keeping him awake. He took some of the pills and was nearly out when the subchief knocked at the door. Mwoya was an important man in the area, chief of the sublocation which lay next to the mission, up the ridge from town. He served on the committee for the Kigeli secondary school where he said little but always gave teachers the impression he was trying to have them fired. He had cousins in important ministries and friends at the Post Office. He knew everything.

He told Hank there was a very sick man who had to get to the hospital but that he was up on the high road where, with all the muck and rain, only a Land Rover could go. Hank, heavy with sleep, beaded curtains of fatigue dangling in his vision, could barely make out the bulky man wrapped in rubber and canvas standing on the stoop in the rain. But he agreed to go, put on his coat, and plucked the car keys off their hook by the side of the door.

Hank was soon completely lost in the storm and the barbiturate daze, and he surrendered himself to Mwoya's directions. Underneath the fresh mud on the road were old corrugations that never disappeared. Between the bouncing and the slipping, the car frame rattled and groaned, and the headlight beam flared in all directions, skidding over the dark green carpet of the small tea farms and the whitewashed earthen walls of the houses, then soaring up against the clouds. As they climbed higher they skirted the edge of the untilled land, the forest, the trees dark against the massy web of vines and the lightening sky with the full moon just beginning to show.

# Kenya, 1971

Mwoya pushed against Hank's shoulder and told him to make a sharp left into what appeared to be an open meadow, the soccer field of a county primary school. As soon as the Land Rover stopped, Mwoya jumped out of the car and ran toward a small crowd. There were forty or fifty people in the field with a group of old women to one side, arms folded across their chests, talking in high-pitched bursts. A larger circle of men stood around one of the goalposts, some carrying pangas, the blades of which flickered and bent in the moon's half-light. Mwoya went up to the men, there was a shout, and the circle opened to admit him.

Hank nodded at the wheel, alone by the path, while a violent discussion in Kigeli floated toward him over the grass. In his years at the station he had never quite learned the language, though it was just at the edge of his understanding, as if he were trying to put together the words of a conversation spoken under water.

A cluster of four or five men broke off from the circle and started walking toward the Land Rover. There was a tall dark man in the center, his face blank in the night. They all seemed to have pangas, and Mwoya, walking to the side, starting, stopping, dancing around the others, kept jabbing the central man in the arms and side with a closed fist. Hank couldn't tell if he was beating him or encouraging him.

They moved closer to the car and Hank finally realized what he hadn't figured out before, that there was no sick man, that Mwoya had lied in order to get the car or to get him. Now he was alone on the mountain with five armed strangers coming at him. Suddenly they were yanking at the doors of his car. The tall figure in the center lurched forward with a snaky halo of panga blades circling its head, and all Hank knew was he had to stop them, to keep them from the car. He let go of the wheel, reared back his fist, and hit through the open window right in the man's face, a good old Tennessee punch.

Then everything was still. The underwater yelling stopped. The mountainside was quiet. Mwoya put one hand on Hank's arm while, with the other, he held up the man in the center, whose hands were tied behind his back. "Do not worry, Mr. Mobley. You are right. This is a bad man."

Hank rubbed his hands and felt the warm blood that covered his knuckles. He looked up at the man's cut lip, saw the frightened face and the black elastic and spectacles that hung around Bob's neck like a loose cleric's collar.

"He is one of your mission boys, I think, Mr. Mobley. The school watchman caught them here and then sent for me. He and my daughter were . . ." The subchief stopped because he didn't know how to say in English what they'd been doing.

The crowd pulled forward and Hank saw the girl in a red school dress standing among the old women, her head bent, fingers waving in her face. She was the daughter of a subchief. It was all out of his hands.

"You will take us now to Kigeli, to the police. They

should deal with the boy." Hank said that he couldn't remember the way, that he was too tired to drive, and he gave Mwoya the keys. Then he got into the back seat, wiped the blood from Bob's face, and held him all the way down the mountain.

At the station, after the police gave Bob the usual beating, Mwoya got Patel's charges revived and Bob was sent to prison at Sungura on Lake Victoria. Hank and Martha went back about their affairs though Hank spent a good deal more time up in the forest shooting with his unregistered shotgun and stuffing the small animals that he killed. The machines still worked for him, but whether through age or indifference he took more time fixing them. He seemed to have lost that edge of earnestness the missionaries required of themselves. After a while, before the stormy season came again, the decision was made to send the Mobleys home.

When Hank, Martha, and Ross had finished and the whole house was packed into a pyramid of boxes out on the lawn, Hank went back through the empty rooms looking for anything left behind. Mostly there were just the old tables and chairs which belonged to the mission. Then he rattled open the rusty padlock of the toolshed he had built and scraped around inside for a few minutes. When he came back around to the front of the house, he was carrying an old battery-operated power saw he'd rigged up for cutting firewood. "I guess you or

# Mobley's Troubles

Beulah can use this if you want to," he told Ross, patting the thing on its wooden handle. "But be careful with it. Just you two. This is a white man's tool, and I don't want anyone else using it, you hear?" The Scotsman took the contraption from him. Hank's voice was hard and his eyes were new—dark and brilliant like a desert sky lit by lightning in the last moment before rain.

# New England, 1988

## On the Flats

Every morning when the weather is fine, I take a walk down Lincoln Street. The views are always gorgeous—Winslow Homer painted several series of watercolors in this neighborhood—but what most reassures me, most convinces me I am home, are the sounds. There are bird cries, some as easily decipherable as an antiphony of robins, one on each side of the street, or the mewing of gulls. Others are harder to figure: complicated rasps and warbles only my wife's family—who know these things—could identify.

In the summer, one can hear the human world as well: the hissing of hoses, doors shutting, the rush of faucets. Always, behind everything, is the surprising sound of the bell buoys' ring, a soft clang, its source invisible, that heightens my sense of how disconnectedly flat and midwestern the frame houses seem, as if not Dorothy, but Kansas, had been drawn up and carried to this cold, northern sea.

Lincoln Street used to be called Masquash Way. The word means "big moose" or "big rock" or big something in the local Indian speech; the last syllable has always been obscure. In any event, after the Civil War, the residents decided that history outranked nature and the name was changed. The road itself used to wander, hugging the coastline, following each of the string of unimportant coves—Goose and Plum and Rock, Streeter's and Miller's—from Eastern Point to the harbor. Now, like a river that has lost its meanders, it plows straight through to the shopping district and, even walking, you catch only glimpses of the shellfish flats that Homer painted, snapping by like postcards.

In the morning the usual walkers and joggers scrape along, mostly retirees and people like myself who don't go to the city to work. Mitchell Streeter, a man I've represented, is always there, setting off. Mitchell is an ambulatory psychotic. When I first heard the expression—eavesdropping on a phone conversation in a doctor's office—it seemed to mean someone who managed to get around in the outside world despite his psychosis. In fact, it turns out to be a person for whom getting around in the outside world *is* his psychosis. Walking is all he does. He goes up and down Lincoln every day, following the same path they use in the Fourth of July mini-marathon, and then goes out to loiter at the traffic circle where the highway comes through. Sometimes he ventures on the shoulder of the Interstate. He never hitchhikes but plods along smoothly with his hands in the pockets of an old army jacket definitely not his own, a short, muscular man in his forties with a face of dissolution and a body as trim as anybody's would be who walked thirty miles a day.

Mitchell frequently gets in trouble with the police, but always in small, mostly self-abusive ways. Our community is enormously tolerant of madmen, a place where the psychiatrist and two of the local policemen take a weekly sauna together. Canons of privacy are only loosely respected and everyone is given the benefit of the doubt.

This tolerance can sometimes become lazy and destructive. Lives of pain are lived here without much notice from the community and not all our local lunatics are as genteel as Mitchell. There are horrible, Gothic figures of genuine evil who live in sleeping bags in the woods at the center of the peninsula in summer, and periodically make the area the scene of fairy-tale murders, Red Riding Hood and Hansel and Gretel killings. To wander alone in the reclaimed pastureland, now turned back to dark forest, can be chancy and foolish.

Mitchell's father, a widower who, by the way, himself is no prize, is not unaware of his son's problems and calls him a bum, a word which now has the archaic ring of terms, like "artisan" and "neurasthenic," derived from outmoded categories. As a lawyer, I am aware that the line between a bum and a crazy is of interest to governmental agencies. Mr. Streeter, however, simply prefers to live in a world of bums rather than crazies. Of course, he is a crazy himself.

My next-door neighbor, Bob Streeter, is no crazy,

though he is distantly related to Mitchell and his father. Bob is a real go-getter. He jogs, but has already been out and back by the time I make my rounds. Bob has great posture which I used to attribute to his army service, but which is apparently the result of a vertebral fusion. He earns his living as an artist and, unlike me, he is always making toys for his kids. I have not made anything out of wood since I fashioned a silent butler in the eighth grade. I do try to point things out for my daughter Laura. I take her for walks in the woods and show her the signs of former habitation: the old foundation holes, hidden among barberry briars and loosestrife, and the ancient roses and parsley that are the remnants of garden plants in the forest. It makes me sad that this may not be as immediately attractive to her as a homemade doll or a wooden boat that floats in the bathtub, but it is what I can do.

Bob Streeter is said to be having an affair with Jennifer Moskowitz-Mason, whom I see on my walks, usually stretched out on the ground in her garden. She talks to her flowers and it seems to work. They are enormously gorgeous and healthy, as—when she stands up—is Jenny herself, a tall, imposing blonde who works as a past-lives therapist in town in a waterfront office not far from my own. Jenny is an Indo-Freudian. She believes that reincarnation opens a vast chain of childhoods to screw one up and is willing to pursue troubles deep into the past. Jenny's school of thought, by being so openly spacey, is less threatening to a lot of local people than more orthodox psycho-therapies. Bob was initially one of her clients, though I believe he stopped seeing her professionally when things started to get more serious.

Because he works at home and because both our wives take the morning train into Boston, Bob and I often share child care. Though we trust each other with our children, he does not confide in me and he has never actually told me about himself and Jennifer, not that he is under any obligation. I suspect Bob feels our wives have forfeited something, a kind of citizen-ship, by going to work in the city and that what we do here—Bob and I, our children, and more to the point, Jenny—takes place in a protected world that our spouses have no right to challenge. He feels a sense of community and, perhaps, one of complicity as well.

For my part I have no great horror of adultery, but no inclination toward it either. I honestly believe there are duties associated not with anything as vague and haughty-sounding as one's position in society, but with one's personality, one's biology. I've always thought that, for me, being a family man is something to be accepted and not chosen, more a zoological ne-cessity than a moral compromise.

I first met Bob Streeter's cousin Mitchell when he came to our door, shortly after we moved in, to sell me a piece of pornographic scrimshaw. What Mitchell really wanted was to borrow money, but he felt he had to offer me something in return. As fewer and fewer men actually go to sea from this peninsula, there seems to be a corresponding increase in the variety of nautical gewgaws. In fact, it made a lot of sense to me that sailors, alone at sea for months at a time with Rorschachian bits of whale teeth in their hands, would do something like this. Mitchell himself had no idea what he was offering. He did not try to point out the workmanship or, on the other hand, to leer. He must have had an attic full of this sort of thing and, when in need, simply reached in to grab the first trinket he could find and auction off.

"Is this for use or admiration?" I asked him, thinking myself clever.

"I could use ten dollars," he told me, and waited. His eyes scanned our living room of still-unpacked boxes and empty teak bookcases. It obviously made no sense to him. I told him I would loan him the money, if he would pay me back, but I didn't want the scrimshaw. "That's no problem," he told me and called me Wilbur, the name of the former owner of our house. I realized, somewhat sheepishly, that while I was intent on teaching him the values of contract and thrift, Mitchell thought I was someone else. His sense of time was broader than my own. Mitchell would be coming back to explain his lack of repayment to others long after I was gone.

"Do you keep all your stuff packed up?" he asked me. Foolishly, I started to explain. "I like that," Mitchell said as he folded the ten and put it in his shoe. "I really like that." He looked around, his astonishment of a moment before turned to an immense satisfaction. He clutched the whale ivory like a blackjack, the point into his hand. "Well, now I must be going," he said, nodding his close-shaven head, not moving an inch. "My father asks after you often."

"Actually, I don't think we've met yet."

"Yes. I'm sorry about that"—he shook his head even more vigorously, since I had just let drop an astounding truth—"it's the least that I can do." We stood for a moment, Mitchell, relaxed now, myself, nervous, afraid he was going to steal something, though of course nothing for him to steal smaller than a chair was yet out in the room. Finally, he said, "Well, now I really must be off," and was gone.

I am terrified of my daughter's adolescence. Laura is only five now but already I have dreams of fistfights on our lawn like those I knew about when I was a teenager: boys struggling over who would get to take out, and worse, the most promising girls, the ones who, according to a little printed book of consequences sent out for our twentieth reunion, have all become aerobics instructors—divorced, fit and inviolate. I see Laura tormented, huddled in an upstairs bedroom, watching the chaos on prom night, the bloodied losers being taken away in rented stretch limousines, the waves crashing out beyond the grass.

# On the Flats

This lawn—the location of my terrified dreams—is the same one that Mitchell's father once drove his car over. Angry or drunk, the old man was reasserting his claim to an ancient pathway that would lead him to the site—now, in fact, underwater—of his cousin's, Bob's father's, house. A month after I had helped push it away from the inlet, the elder Streeter accused his son of stealing the car. Actually, Mitchell had merely driven it until he ran out of gas in western Massachusetts, where he got out and began walking back here—two hundred miles. The state troopers found him and sent him home on the bus, in the custody of a deputy. Meanwhile, they impounded the car and Mr. Streeter had to go out to the Berkshires to retrieve it. While his father was gone, Mitchell was released, went home, and took his father's bicycle, with a jerry can of gas strapped to the rack, onto the road to get the car himself. Local police united the two in Worcester. Mr. Streeter, bitten by remorse, retained me to defend Mitchell on the stolen car charge that he himself had filed. I had the case continued and got them into family counseling.

Representing Mitchell, even for just a week, unsettled me. I examined my own family relations. When I was small my father traveled on business a great deal and he once jumped out of a burning small plane, on the ground, rescuing the pilot, only to get on another plane twenty minutes later. I still see this ridiculous gesture in my dreams, the way my daughter repeatedly watches on the VCR the scene in *Dumbo* where the elephant child stands in panic in the burning building, surrounded by maliciously incompetent clowns. She rewinds the tape to see the miracle of the earflaps, the perennial rescue. I see only the foolish re-entry into the flames, the animal trapped in the fire again and again without knowledge or experience. Why do we continue to go back and forth, I wonder. Why don't we exercise judgment when we can?

Bob Streeter is not a good painter, but he is very successful. He does the kind of conservative seascapes that the local Art Association gives awards for: lobster pots, fishermen seated with tools in their hands, little dots of color. A cloudy day, a touch of foam. No faces. These things sell like hotcakes and because of them there are more people on this thin neck of land who actually make a living as artists than in most big cities. Bob has a large studio in the house and, since he is more tolerant of noise than I am, he can have the kids playing in a corner with their own brushes, daubing while he concentrates. I try to do the same, hooked up by modem to my office, when I don't have to meet with clients, but it rarely works. The kids need questions answered, fights adjudicated, hands and mouths cleaned. My daughter gets her tiger ears stuck on her head. I pay attention to these things. I suspect Bob does not.

It will all end—the juggling of work at home, the

sharing with Bob—next year. Our children will probably go to one of the private schools, although, having grown up in the Midwest, where people learn to be friendly and attend public school, I was taught that private schools are for delinquents. Our local public system, however, is terrible. The roofs leak and the teachers have become beaten down, hostile and cynical. My wife, who is from this area, went to an excellent public school that has now been turned into housing for the elderly. I want my daughter to have the kind of experiences you get in a public school and meet the different sorts of people who live in town. Perhaps, like many of the middle-class teenagers, Laura eventually could work in one of the fish-packing plants for the summer. In the tones of her speech and her odd local adjectives, she has already, without effort, acquired Bob Streeter's sense of community, his inner map. Laura is, after all, a native. She has the capacity to get along.

One morning, late in August, she came to my desk in the study and asked permission to go for a boat ride with Mr. Streeter. Bob takes the children out often, in a red dinghy that he made himself, naturally, without nails or any other kind of metal. I checked the weather—light, puffy clouds, a low, pleasant wind—and, reminding Laura to wear her life jacket, granted her request.

A few minutes later I watched the red rowboat making its way out across the shining water, the steady-dipping oars black against the light. The space between the back windows of our houses and the shellfish flats is a vast plain where the water, even at the highest tide, never gets more than a few feet deep. Its impracticality for navigation lends to its consideration as an aesthetic object. On still days, it can seem purely ornamental, a reflecting pool like those at the Taj Mahal and the Washington Monument, places where wading or gliding in a shallow boat becomes a subversive act, as much because it destroys an object of contemplation as because it violates local ordinance. Of course there are no laws against rippling the water here, but you can understand why the tide is never running in Homer's watercolors, why the skiffs lie still and the clam diggers are stopped for a moment in their toil. With their bodies bent over and hats obscuring their faces, their skin and the white of their clothes are, like the empty anchored boats, always mirrored quietly in the tidal pool. As I've said, the figures in Bob's paintings don't have faces either, but there's a difference. Bob is just painting light as he has been taught. He can't see the faces. They are too far away or the sun is too strong. Faces do not occur to Bob. With Homer, the blanks where there should be features are a conscious choice, a sacrifice to an idea of beauty, perhaps, or a touch of the artist's imperial malice. Bob, on the other hand, paints what he sees. He has no secrets.

The red dinghy drew up on the edge of the flats as I watched, the sand gray and wet in the flow of tide. Bob, nothing more than a silhouette, the bottom of some kind of slicker flapping behind his legs, pulled the bow onto the rise while Laura—a swollen munchkin shape in her vest—stood at the side. The Streeter kids must have gone to their grandparents; Bob and Laura were alone. Bob reached into the boat and picked a dark object from the floor—a buoy or a bucket. I hoped he was not intending to dig. The flats up to Ipswich had been closed to shellfishing for months on account of the Red Tide. He pulled more shapes from the boat: a shovel, a long rake, probably—from the distance, it looked more like a spear—then a broom, something, a criminal's tools, I couldn't make them out.

"Do you know Mitchell has Laura out on the boat?"

Jenny Moskowitz-Mason, close to me, looked even more statuesque than usual. She had come straight in, without knocking, and leaned against the desk beside my chair, the skin of her legs cool and troubling to my arm as she peered out the window. She was wearing white tennis shorts and some kind of dinosaur tee shirt, her hair pulled back with a barrette. The button at her waist was loose.

"Mitchell?"

"Bob was with me. In the studio. He just took the boat." She was barefoot and there was a cut above her left ankle as if she had been running through briars.

"Was he being hostile?"

"Bob or Mitchell?" Jenny was wary, she sensed an intrusion.

"I meant Mitchell."

"How can one tell? We just saw it. I thought you should know."

"He did ask my permission. Or he let Laura come in and ask." I turned off my typewriter and senselessly started to stack statute books on the desk.

"Mitchell isn't really a hostile person," she said.

"No, he's not."

Jenny was trying to calm me down. She turned her head to look directly at me, questioning. There were faint drops of sweat where the hair was drawn back above her ear. "You'd better go get her."

"I don't have a boat."

"It's not very deep."

"No, it's not." I started to move to the back porch and down to the water, stepped into a pair of rubber sandals, and then, thinking better of it, hopped out of them at the edge of the deck and rolled up the legs of my pants. "Why didn't Bob go after them?"

"I told you. We just saw it through the studio window. Bob thought it was your responsibility." Irritated, Jenny was having trouble keeping up. She appeared to be limping. "We didn't know if you'd given them permission."

"I had."

I left her on the deck and jumped down over the low wall of bricks to the water. She stood there, peering out with her hand above her eyes, the image of one of the old captains' wives. Her obvious generosity of intention upset me. Wasn't she angry that I'd interrupted her tryst by having my daughter kidnapped by a madman? I plowed my way through the soft sucking sand, the water at my knees.

Of what exactly was I afraid? Red Tide? Assault? Of course, as Jenny had told me, Mitchell didn't harm people, but he didn't help them either. One had to give unceasingly to people like Mitchell. The fact was they tired me. Mitchell tired me, Bob, hidden somewhere, watching, tired me, Jenny tired me, even my daughter tired me. I was being responsible, wading steady through the inlet, messing up Homer's still waters, sinking in resentment.

I drew nearer to Mitchell and Laura, but what they were doing was no clearer to me. Laura was sitting on the rail of the red dinghy, trailing her toes in the water, while Mitchell, a pointless sou'wester on his head, dug with his shovel. It was definitely a shovel—the bag of murderer's tools had dissolved to the usual equipment—but he wasn't extracting anything from the sand, merely piling the petty dredgings next to him. If anything, he seemed to be returning dark shapes to the ground, sowing rocks, planting bulbs. I looked back to the houses and could see Jenny, still on the dock, gazing first at us and then, searching, back to Bob's house. Where was he? Why hadn't he come? I imagined him in his studio or in his bedroom, dressed, naked, contemptuous, embarrassed, watching me, shielded by the bright sun's reflection.

When Mitchell finally saw me coming, he froze, his arms spread, the rake clutched straight like a staff, a scarecrow's silhouette. He waited that way while I pushed through the cold tide for three or four minutes. Laura stopped her play. I was spreading immobility, making her afraid.

"You're not going to eat anything, are you?" It was ridiculous, all I could think of to say as I arrived. Laura stared at me, dumbfounded.

"They're from Maine. They're clean." Mitchell started into rapid motion to defend himself. He reached into his pail and held up a puffed plastic plate oozing bivalves, the shrink-wrap ripped from the top. He was carefully burying a bucket of clams from the Stop and Shop.

"That won't do any good, Mitchell, the disease is in the water."

"No, you'll see. They'll grow and spread." I was offending him. He reached back into the bucket. "I brought deodorant, too."

"What for?"

"For the smell."

"Mr. Streeter is silly, Daddy." Laura began to kick again, then hopped off the boat and walked to us. She lifted one of the supermarket clams and tried to squeeze from it a response.

I turned to Mitchell. "I think you should go in."

"Well, perhaps I should, but I can't."

"You can't?"

"I'm stuck. I'm stuck in the muck." He began to laugh, at first just friendly, conciliatory giggles, then in wider and deeper breaths, drawing in all the air he could manage, a soft blow of panic underneath a pile of sound. The rising tide had darkened and soddened the sand and Mitchell had, in fact, sunk a few inches into the flat. But his laughter, now a kind of long moan, and the bellowing of his abdomen—underneath the flagrant yellow slicker he was wearing only a pair of gym shorts—bore no proportion to his slight shift of equilibrium.

"Just lift your feet slowly."

"I can't." He began to rock his head and upper body, back and forth, his legs braced, pointlessly paralyzed from the waist down. The rake, still clutched in his hand, swung wildly in the air. The dread in Mitchell's face was greater than any terror of quicksand. It was as if he were afraid he would never move again, but be imprisoned forever in the flats like one of those faceless, sexless models of Homer's, rendered permanently anonymous.

I pulled the rake from his grip and clutched Mitchell around the middle, tugging his feet from the suction. We bumped foreheads, pushing his cap off and down to where the creeping tide could catch it. With an increasing hatred, I imagined Jenny and Bob at their observation posts, taking it all in. Mitchell, in his terror, contributed nothing. He was pure burden, a graceless strength pulling me down. Laura grabbed my belt and I melted in gratitude as we accomplished the last few inches to free Mitchell's toes.

The wind blew suddenly cold. Mitchell walked in little circles on the bar, now everywhere an inch or two underneath the running tide. His legs vibrated in the tremors of whatever drug the doctors were forcing him to take.

"Now," he said, "I'll leave." His eyes followed his hat, floating up the inlet, as if it were a treacherous pet that had wandered.

I wanted to leave him there to fend for himself, to pick my daughter up, take her to the dinghy, and row in over this false sea to our house. Of course, I couldn't. He was crazy. He would panic again. He would drown in the shallows.

Laura was afraid now, the water creeping up her ankles, the clouds in the sky somehow lower. I was going to have to play St. Christopher and carry her the five hundred feet across the inlet while Mitchell took the boat in.

Far across the water, I could hear a chainsaw buzz. Bob stood at the edge of his own lawn. His white shorts, his ramrod back were all I could see, he and his Jennifer a neat pair.

"I'm fine, really I am." There was a predictable surprise now at the end of each of Mitchell's sentences, the last second thinned and upbeat, catching the tremor of his limbs.

I started to give orders. "Go in the boat, Mitchell. I'll push you off. Don't be afraid."

"But where are the oars?" He looked at his hands, wonders.

"Right there. I'll push you off in the right direction.

# On the Flats

The tide will carry you in." He had nothing to do but follow the flow that would bend him toward the land.

"Thank you. Thank you." He made no move to the oars, but laid his hands limply on his lap as he sat on the thwart. He screwed his head back as I ran him off the bar. "My father says you should always say thank you when people do good things," he confided to Laura, an instruction, a secret. I was left with my little girl holding tight to my leg, the tide pushing at us.

Mitchell, running with the tide, racing to the shore, didn't even have to row. "I won't get stuck, will I? I don't want to get stuck," he yelled to us, the same terrible catch in his throat. Then he waved—a soft, perfunctory, good morning wave—and I waved back, a nod, a reassuring smile. This was all good cheer now, in order to avert catastrophe. The boat flowed in gracefully, tugged to a slight turn at the gentle channel in the middle of the inlet, then, puffed along like a child's paper vessel, it brushed forward toward the sloping lawns. Mitchell, easing to land, had turned his waves from us to Bob and Jenny who, now that the die was cast, had both jumped into the water. They were broadcasting greeting, a warmth of welcome, splashes of celebration, drawing in the lunatic to the bosom of his family.

As it drew near, Bob grabbed the dinghy's line and hauled: the artist unwilling to let go of his creation. The three of them settled into peaceful procession. With one hand Bob towed his cousin—in state in the skiff—and with the other, he met Jenny's outstretched fingers. Gently, five hundred yards from me, they walked on water.

At sea on the flats, I was scared my daughter was learning that I didn't like everybody, a small, forlorn secret she probably already knew. But there was more. I felt I was glowing harm. I could sense the heat in my arms, in my thighs, in the muscles of my jaw. Pillared in the sand, my daughter clinging to my leg, I was certain that even all the artistic water washing at our feet could never cool my heightened, dangerous temperature. I stood on the bar, ready to carry my daughter home, steadfast and full of rancor.

# Kenya, 1980

## A Good White Hunter

Atherton was from somewhere else. Sometimes he could barely remember where. Barrow, he would say, or Bolton, names from a hat. The names all meant the same to the Kigeli. An Englishman, they would think, an *mzungu.*

Occasionally he did get letters from home, a cousin who tried to keep in touch and sent him newspaper clippings. A doctor's family had moved into the small Midlands town, with unemployed relatives and strange cooking odors, and the editors were worried about being overrun by Pakistani hordes. Atherton had never written back about his own marriages to African women, his black children. He'd never written back at all.

Atherton had three wives. The first was a matter of love and need. The others, from his point of view, were hardly intentional, a confusing set of obligations he had fallen upon the way a lizard might walk into a child's banana-leaf snare, for lack of adequate peripheral vision.

# Kenya, 1980

He had been married to Rebekah Ndaru barely a year when the first young cousin had returned from Nairobi to their home district, pregnant and ashamed. He had been told by his in-laws in a ceremonious council of sugar beer and ancient milk—the same vile substance that, stored for months in a gourd, always seemed to Atherton to presage some disastrous family duty—that the child would need a father. They did not tell him directly that he was to be that father. Rebekah told him that herself in his bed. The cousin had already promised she would always show deference to the elder wife and she could be of use to the household. She could help in the fields, digging and weeding. The girl had said she would never return to the city.

Atherton hadn't the slightest notion how to make such a decision. He didn't know what was allowed and what was forbidden. He didn't know if he really had any choice at all. Was he permitted to feel imposed upon? Threatened? Upset? Was he permitted to covet the young girl's body?

Atherton did covet the young girl's body. It was the hormonal fullness of her pregnancy, the shining luster of her skin, that tipped the balance for him. He dreamed of other children, his own, running through the tall grass of the compound. It was all addled together in his mind: the promise of new sex, the taste of sour milk, the starting of a dynasty.

In the meantime, his kingdom was close to disaster. The corrugated tin of Rebekah's roof leaked and there were rats in his own house. A man from the Government had convinced him to grow something called macadamia nuts on his land without telling him that it would take five years for the things to yield. Atherton had gone to Nairobi looking for work but the capital was now full of other white men, birds of passage, with more education than he could ever hope for, briefcases full of degrees and qualifications. They worked for the Government and the UN and an incomprehensible host of international commissions. They had their own bars and their own bar girls and cash flowed through their fingers.

Atherton did know something about animals. He had been able to hunt and shoot when that was still a viable option. He was not a great white hunter, he would tell the tourists, but he was a good white hunter. But all hunting was illegal now. Sid Landers, an older man, born in Kenya, had suggested Atherton apply for a grant. That was where the money and the action were nowadays—universities and societies for the preservation of something or other that were willing to offer money to study the game. Sitting in a blind, taking notes on gazelle behavior: it did not seem all that taxing. But when Atherton actually confronted the necessary papers, the application was more terrifying than any leopard. He read it line by line and he could feel his heart racing and the sweat coating his palms. There was no way he could compete with some American graduate student who had the schooling and the proper words. Atherton didn't even own a type-writer. He let the forms die and the deadline pass.

The dream of work in Nairobi faded. Atherton returned to the provinces. In the small market towns like Kigeli, he could sell his labor to the Africans and Indians who owned the gas stations and the feed stores. They were willing to pay him, he knew, just to see a white man unloading their truck or working behind the counter selling matches and tins of condensed milk, quiet and deferring, an inexpensive badge of status for successful merchants. Then the second pregnant young cousin returned to Atherton's *shamba*, this time from Mombasa with a story about an American sailor. There was another cut-rate *baraza* with his in-laws: more sugar beer, old milk, and another marriage. With a sense of doom, Atherton paid the necessary goats for the severely discounted bride-price and took the new wife into his bed. In the market clearing, he watched the oxen pushing the long bamboo spokes of the sugar-cane press and felt the same yoke on his neck, the same slow walk in endless circles.

The young wives came to him in turn, walking across the grass in the cool air with thin shifts on their shoulders and a smoldering candle-lantern in their hands. With the new children that kept coming after the nights of thrashing on the thin rope cot, Atherton let his beard grow long, his hair shaggy. In his mind, the hairiness had something to do with virility, and with race as well. Not that he cared that much about racial differences. He cared and he didn't care, but the African men were simply not as hairy as he was. They no doubt saw his facial furriness as something odd and extravagant, something animalian, a link to lower orders.

But there were benefits, too. Atherton was convinced of this. It was tied in with the matter of hats. Sid Landers, who had children of his own by Kenyan women, said that hats were crucial, that the African children were just as lively and intelligent as the Europeans in the first year or two of life, but then the sun set in. The bones of the skull closed more slowly in the African, Landers said, and until the bones hardened, the brain was exposed in the gaps with only a thin layer of skin and the nappy hair for protection. Landers thought there wasn't enough coverage from the tightly curled hair. The sun's rays could dull the brain and stop the growth, especially in the thin air of the highlands. Thick hats were needed; Landers recommended fur felt.

Atherton did not want to take chances with his children. He included without a second thought the two siblings of mysterious fathering. He could do nothing about the speed at which their skulls closed, but he could get them the hats. They were made of a cheap, mottled green fabric and were the clearest, perhaps the only, evidence of the children's semi-European extraction. The dark skin, the hair and lips, of his sons and daughters were much more Kenyan than English.

There was little to distinguish them, except the hats, from their playmates in neighboring *shambas*. Atherton had waited for signs of unusual intelligence in the brood—a longer attention span, some strange new facility—but as the years went by he had strained to see anything out of the ordinary. He thought that, perhaps, was his own defect, his own lack of training. It made him even keener to educate his children. But now, as he stood one Sunday in June, passing an Asian shopkeeper's grain sacks from Land Rover to storeroom, he knew he hadn't a fraction of the money he needed to pay the school fees of twelve sons and daughters.

After his labor, with the sun about to start its quick descent, Atherton washed his hands at a tap in the yard and walked up the wooden steps to Bimji's office for his pay. The storekeeper, a heavy man with hooded eyes, sat at an improbable oak desk that dripped papers and chips of ancient yellow paint. He had an improvised strongroom in the office, really no more than a closet, into which he disappeared for a minute before returning with a cash box. Bimji counted out Atherton's bills from a stack of worn currency, and then a smaller pile for Guantai, the night watchman, who, leaning on a staff, waited patiently in line behind the white man.

The twilight cool was beginning as Atherton walked down the wooded road toward the Higher School compound. Shreds of mist were joining in the low spots: the ravine below the prison, the valley folds that stretched over the mountainside, outward and down, to the desert lands far below. Atherton pulled the stained flaps of his safari jacket—a hand-tailored remnant from his hopeful first years in the country—up against his neck and the scratchy bottom of his beard. The breeze at his back, he rounded a corner into the cluster of neatly trimmed homes and propped himself against a hedge below the window where the Missionary Lady was undressing.

Her name was Thompson or Thomas, something like that. Atherton had asked once, then found it more satisfying to be left vague. A teacher at the Girls' School, she still dressed methodically for dinner, standing oblivious before the open curtain, confident in that neighborhood of schools and the old church that everyone, of whatever color, was deeply religious. As she changed her bra and panties, the white woman patted herself dry from the day's heat with some kind of powder. Atherton imagined he could smell its perfume through the window. He followed her hands with his eyes, along the smooth flow of her skin, to the join of her legs.

Physical love was becoming something of a sore point with Atherton. Keeping three wives happy, he would tell fellow drinkers at the Coffee Hotel bar—with appropriate coughs and what he felt was a wry and knowing smile—was a bed matter, especially with African women. He would gesture to a corner where Webber sat nursing a Scotch, a textbook example of the difficulty. The Canadian teacher was married to a Kenyan woman, a Somali with a dazzling face and elegant carriage, who, as Headmistress of the Girls' school, was brilliant and powerful as well. One look at the man, a red-haired, weary-eyed, emaciated stick of nervous energy, illustrated the problem. It was what happened when university degrees married each other, Atherton would say, then nod slowly over his pint.

But Atherton's own wives, however relentlessly satisfied he imagined them, were two hundred miles away. They had turned him into a kind of migrant worker, like the miserable bastards who would go off to the mines somewhere and dutifully send their paychecks home. He understood their desires. His women wanted a normal life: a *shamba*, a small house for each wife that wouldn't wash away in the rains, children, friends in the compound. They wanted everything he could supply, except himself. So they had contrived to send him off to a quiet hellhole like Kigeli where he slept in a rented shack and fed himself out of bars and cheap hotels.

The thought was unfair and Atherton knew it. He was not any worse off than any of a hundred other men. Everyone chased money over the hillsides, living—or hoping to live—in one place and working—or trying to work—somewhere else. At least he had a bit of land for his family. A drunken white settler moaning over the end of Empire had given his entire farm to Atherton in the bar of the Norfolk Hotel a week after the country's independence. It was seven hundred acres of highland wheat fields and the settler, in a quite self-conscious gesture of despair, had thrown it away on a working-class youngster just over from England. Unfortunately for Atherton's future, the settler had sobered up in the morning and discovered that legions of blacks were not going to overrun his property. On the contrary, if he wanted to leave, the Government was willing to buy his land at the market rate. The settler took them up on it and, guiltily remembering the boy at the Norfolk, carved out two acres for Atherton on the edge of a liana-strangled ravine. It would make a good house lot, he said. That was how Atherton, contriving a truck garden and a patch of coffee, became a landowner and a bachelor eligible enough for Rebekah Ndaru's family to consider, all while still unemployed.

The Missionary Lady buttoned the last of her garments and reached up, fully clothed, to twist off the bare bulb that lit her bedroom. Atherton breathed quietly for a moment in the darkness under the hedge where he sat. Then he stood up, brushed the yew needles from his jacket, and walked back to the main road.

Atherton had never considered crime an open option until that night. To have to steal money from his employer to pay his children's school fees was deeply embarrassing to him. It was shameful, he felt, until he realized that thinking in terms of shame, as if his every action were done in some public display, paraded before his in-laws and the man in the street, was African thinking. It was a sign that—in the missionaries' sniffing phrase—he was going native. Atherton despised the people who thought that way, but he knew there was some truth to the idea. No one was going to watch. If he were going to steal successfully, it had damn well better not be in public. Here in Kigeli, away from his wives, away from his children, away from anyone Atherton knew, he should at least be able to take advantage of his own loneliness.

And no one would show great sympathy to Bimji. The Indian storekeeper would have been hated, if he had been considered human. As it was he was merely wondered at, an uncouth, large-mouthed, fairy-tale dragon who stood at the gate between the Kigeli and the basic necessities of life. If you wanted a radio in Kigeli or a flashlight battery, a cigarette or a can of butter, a case of beer or a gallon of gasoline, you had to go through the Asian. He sold everything and had become the subject of local myth. He was said to dabble in poaching, his cellars piled with elephant tusks and leopard hides. He was wifeless and the late-night men of Kigeli, who wandered the streets sipping from Coke bottles full of sugar beer, swore that Land Rovers carrying kohl-eyed Indian boys emptied before Bimji's house in the hours before dawn.

But distaste and suspicion for the victim would not exempt Atherton from penalty if he were caught. The police were bastards, but he would rather be in their hands than trapped by the casual, nearly thoughtless, rage for criminal justice of the average Kigeli. There were no murders among the Kigeli, but there were executions. Atherton had once seen twenty grown men leaping on a hapless teenage shoplifter, smashing his face with sticks and fists. The watchmen of the town, who seemed to spend their whole lives curled in doorways asleep or squatting on their hams before banked coal fires, could wake to a howling viciousness at the cry of "Thief!" Still, the vision of the door to Bimji's strongroom, blackness beyond, flickered in his mind.

Atherton began to study Guantai's movements. The watchman was at least twenty years older than Atherton. Like all the other Kigeli of his profession, he wore a woolen skullcap and an old British Army trenchcoat, the collar pulled up, in even the hottest weather. He was said to have been a Mau-Mau before Independence, a fighter in the forest. But that was a claim most would-be watchmen made to add cachet to their resumes. Storekeepers wanted a savage or a guerrilla at the door. They needed cutthroats and what they got were aged men of ambiguous strength, a corps of parallel hermits.

The skin of Guantai's hands was gray. He wore long, dangling earflaps—the legacy of a tribal youth—folded up and over the tops of his ears. Atherton had no idea where the watchman lived or how he spent his days. He would appear every afternoon in front of Bimji's store with a staff and a sharpened panga, then, by the first hour after dawn, dissolve again into the streets.

# Kenya, 1980

Atherton bought a Japanese watch from Bimji and began to time everything—when Guantai arrived, how long he took to eat the evening meal he brought with him in a battered stewpot, when he lit his fire, when he stretched his legs. The African seemed to spend endless hours staring at things. He would gaze unblinking at the stars, the silhouette of the mountain peak in the moonlight, the vibrating darkness along the hedge that ran behind the row of shops.

For a week Atherton sat opposite Guantai on the wooden sidewalk that lined Kigeli's main street. The two men were in full view of each other, but there was nothing unusual in that. Besides the corps of watchmen, the night streets held the regular drunks and the landless men who wandered the open, grassy square where, by day, women spread their onions and bananas on blankets for sale. At any given moment, fifteen men could be sitting in front of the shops on Bimji's street, each staring at a bottle or the ground, silent with each other while the tin, creaking sounds of Congo music flowed out of the bars. Guantai acknowledged the white man's presence with a wave of his hand. He seemed to suspect nothing.

Back in his room, Atherton listened to combination locks. An ironmonger sold him a pile of the rusty hardware, by weight, and the Englishmen practiced with them, straining to hear the falling of the tumblers. If he could somehow get into the store around Guantai, he would have only to pry the strongroom door and unlock the Indian's cash box before slipping back out.

Atherton chose a Tuesday night for his job, then changed his mind. He wanted to extend the process. He was beginning to enjoy the planning, the conspiring with himself. Day after day he plotted, in his room, while laboring in the backs of trucks, even at the twilight rendezvous in the Missionary Lady's hedge. The necessary calculations filled his mind. He found a satisfaction in identifying the small steps of the watchman's life. With Guantai, the Englishman breathed on the cooking fire, nibbled the ears of salty corn, and stared at the night.

But however much delight he found in contemplating the crime, and whatever fear he had of performing it, Atherton had to get the money before the start of the next school term, two weeks away. He finally settled on a Sunday evening for the attempt. Webber's wife had scheduled a joint schools production of *A Midsummer Night's Dream*, which was likely to siphon off some of the street traffic. Atherton had his doubts whether Shakespeare was really likely to attract the prospective vigilantes he was worried about. Still, there was some talk about the drama, and the twin girls who were to play Hermia and Helena, in the Coffee Hotel restaurant where he took his dinners. Even if only the town's four policemen attended the production—and for complicated political reasons he only dimly understood, they might be required to—it would be a help.

Atherton had calculated that Guantai went out to

relieve himself seven times every night. It seemed to the Englishman excessive, but the toothless watchman was old and, as each night wore on, drank more heavily from the gin bottles that formed part of his salary from Bimji. The privy was nothing more than a trench behind an *mbati* blind—a rectangle of corrugated tin, propped by a few boards, that stood at the far end of the block of wooden storefronts. The trick would be to break into Bimji's office through the high window that opened above the desk at the back of the Asian's shop, and then, once inside, to keep quiet.

Sunday night came. Atherton blackened his face and arms with charcoal. He fashioned a rough mask from a piece of rag that, even after he washed it for the purpose, still had a choking odor of motor oil clinging to it. Finally, for lack of any other suitable disguise, he wore his safari jacket inside out. Atherton realized the outfit made him look like one of the local madmen, the Africans with malaria-gnawed brains who wore dead flowers in their hair and listened to cardboard radios. Still, he hoped he would look more bizarre than identifiable.

The night was sufficiently dark. By nine o'clock the moon was lost behind the mountain. From where Atherton hid, in a small plot of banana trees along the one paved road that led out of Kigeli, he could see the full two-block length of the town's main street. The bars had seemed to empty some just before the start of the school drama. At least, the street was relatively quiet. The only men visible to the white man were the watchmen. Guantai and his fellows hunkered in front of their *jikos*, the blackened pots of flame before each shop forming two lines of pointed fire down the street. For an instant, Atherton remembered the runway beacons at Nairobi and the plane that had carried him to Africa from his futureless homeland. Then he rose, grabbed a pair of bananas from the tree above him to stuff into his pants pocket, and made his move.

Atherton crossed the paved road in a pool of shadow a hundred yards beyond Kigeli's one electric beacon, the flood that lit the dragon on Bimji's Agip gas station. He slipped through the chickenshit-crusted shanty yards that sided the market square and threw himself to the ground behind the hedge in back of the main street shops. He was already panting. His hands were already cold.

Atherton bellied over, as quietly as he could, to a spot where he could look underneath the hedge. Barely a dozen feet away, he could see the back window to Bimji's office reflecting the night's dim starlight. He could hear Guantai singing a low chant to himself, in front of the store, but he couldn't see the watchman. If he was going to know when the old man went to the privy he would somehow have to get closer, into the narrow, grassy walkway that separated Bimji's shop from its neighbor.

Atherton began to scrape at the dirt beneath his chest. The only quiet way through the hedge would be under it. Fifteen minutes later, the red dirt jammed into his nails, he wriggled through the gap at the base of two bushes into Bimji's storeyard, stepped gingerly around the piles of Chinese cookware and old Land Rover fenders, and made his way to the grassy passage. He slumped against the far wall in a spot where he could observe the watchman and still remain unseen from the street.

Guantai had barely moved since the time Atherton had last seen him, nearly forty-five minutes before. The low Kigeli chant was still on the watchman's lips, half-spoken, half-sung. With his staff, he rapped the short metal legs of the flaming *jiko* in rhythm with the song. The cookfire's shadows—the staff, the flap of Guantai's trenchcoat, the ear of corn in his hand that swelled to an immense club—played across the wall just feet in front of the Englishman. The watchman's gin bottle stood warming by his bare feet. Every minute or so, breaking his song, he took a slow, methodical pull of the liquor, his lips lingering on the glass.

Finally, after Atherton's own bladder had began to nag him uncomfortably, Guantai suddenly shook his head from side to side, pulled himself up with his staff, and shuffled away toward the privy. Atherton broke to the back yard, looked about wildly, then grabbed the bananas from his pocket and smashed the corner pane of Bimji's office window. He clutched at the latch, swung the screenless window open, and pulled himself up and over.

# A Good White Hunter

The Asian's office seemed to glow in the dark. The streaks of yellow on Bimji's desk, the fading sweeps of whitewash on the walls, even the thick red polish on the cement floor pulsed in the near-blackness. Atherton's eyes buzzed. He pulled the rag mask, with its faint, sick smell of oil, down to his neck and taking off his shoes, padded to the door behind the shopkeeper's desk.

The strongroom door gave at once to the Englishman's shoulder. The ease unnerved Atherton. This was all going wrong, he told himself. He should have planned some way to know when Guantai returned from the privy, some way to see. Fumbling, he lit a kerosene lantern that stood on the windowless closet's one small table, then paused to stop the trembling of his hands.

The lantern, the table, the cash box pushed against the wall, nothing else. The austerity dismayed Atherton. He did not know what he had expected—piles of skins from Bimji's supposed poaching, perhaps, a cache of jewelry—but some hidden luxuriance, some secret, guilty wealth. Instead, he found a lightless monk's cell, barely different from his own rented room.

And a cash box with a pick-proof, keyed lock. There would be no combinations, no tumblers to hear fall, only a smooth steel padlock that took some insane and special cylindrical key. Panic began to fill Atherton. He had never actually seen the cash box locked before. He had just assumed that Bimji used the best of the locks the Asian himself sold—the West German ones with the combination dials—not something private.

From outside Bimji's office, Atherton heard scrapings, shreds of music, the creaking of wood. He tried to quiet himself, with Guantai, sure to have returned from his call of nature, now no more than twenty feet away through the walls. Yet his heart pounded still; the breath in his throat raced.

Atherton raised the cash box above his head and studied it. He felt ashamedly like an ape thrown some new toy. The lock itself was hopeless and the edges tight and secure. The only way in would be to saw the bolt, if he had a saw, or simply smash the whole bloody mess open without making a sound. He put the box back on the table and gently tried to lift the lid. In the flickering light he could not be sure, but there seemed to be some give.

A crazy adrenaline confidence returned to Atherton. Holding his breath, he pressed the box between his elbows and began to pull it apart with all his strength, straining, even after he was certain his fingertips were bleeding, pulling with every ounce of his arms' muscle, but quietly, and still tearing, as if his whole body was split in two, until the moment he dropped the box on his unprotected toes.

The shout brought Guantai at once. Atherton could hear the footsteps into the shop, behind the counter, into the office, at the desk, behind him. He didn't care. Huddled over, clutching his wounded foot, Atherton saw himself for an instant, not trapped in the Asian's secret cell, but riding down the road in a limousine, like a government official. Except the flag on his bumper was neither the Kenyan banner nor the Union Jack. All he could make out was a private stain of color: a flag of his own, threatening, indecipherable. In pain, blinking, Atherton lifted his head to Guantai.

The watchman stood above him, a flashlight in one hand, the staff in the other. A sharpened *panga* swung in the trenchcoat's canvas belt.

"Mr. Atherton?" The old Mau-Mau was speaking English, the words softened by alcohol and his toothless gums into something deferential, apologetic.

"Yes. Why yes, I . . ."

"What are you doing? It is not good."

Atherton realized that he was as much stunned by the fact of conversation as by being caught. It occurred to him that he hardly ever spoke to anyone in Kigeli.

"Well, I . . ."

"Wait." Guantai vanished.

Atherton knew there was no point to running now that he had been discovered. The cry would be up. Besides, he realized with a sinking feeling, he didn't know how much weight his foot could take. He picked up the cash box from the floor—still intact—and replaced it carefully on the table.

There was something to be said for prison. The Provincial cells were just down the road, spread along a high plateau beside the ravine. Every evening, in his walks to and from the mission hedge, he could see the smoke curling from the cook fires. The wives of the prisoners prepared their husbands' dinners in the vacant land beyond the barbed wire fence, boiling millet and vegetables in open *sufarias* while the convicts' children clung to their mothers' skirts. They would all be a bloody sight closer together than they were now, Atherton sighed, and, for a change, someone would be taking care of him.

"Come out, *muguru*."

Atherton heard the words from somewhere in the Asian's office. He limped out of the small strongroom and stood beside the yellow-streaked desk.

"All the way, *muguru*." Again, Guantai, disembodied, used the Kigeli term of address—man, age-mate, brother. One of us. "Outside."

Finally, Atherton saw the old man through the broken window.

The watchman was back in Bimji's yard now with five of the other guards: the same bare legs, the same baggy trenchcoats, the same staffs and *pangas*. Atherton swung away the glass and crawled through the office window. He lowered himself to the ground, wincing as the wounded toes touched the earth.

The aged African faces circled about him.

"You should not be a greedy man, *muguru*, you should show respect." Guantai pounded the red dirt with his staff. The last things Atherton saw, before losing consciousness, were the other staffs raised high and the shining flats of the *panga* blades, catching starlight, as the old men closed in.

When he awoke, Atherton was in the forest, his head resting on a cushion of pine needles and wild banana leaves. He could feel the bruises covering his body. His ribs ached; his mouth tasted of salt. He tried to pull himself up, felt a stabbing pain in the back of his head, then paused to rest. The full force of the morning light struck him, even through the leaf canopy above. The sun was already climbing.

Atherton rolled up his sleeves past the dried, cracking stains of blood and studied the mounds of purple swelling on his arms. The memory of the night before was clear in his mind. He would go to prison now. It was all for the best. He rose again, this time more slowly, and searched for a way out of the trees. Somewhere to his right were the town's morning sounds: the punctuated, repetitive whine of a backhoe working, the muffled ringing of truckloads, poorly fastened, making turns on gravel roads. Atherton walked toward the sound and brighter light and noticed someone had put his shoes back on his feet.

A vain impulse to make himself presentable took hold of Atherton. From where he found himself, it was no more than a hundred feet, through a blind of bougainvillea, to the road that led from the Kigeli shops to the mission schools. He tried to straighten his hair and to adjust his jacket which, oddly, was again right side out. The Kamba policeman who supervised what passed for Kigeli's rush hour would be standing in the road before Bimji's Agip station. The watchmen would surely have told him.

Through his mass of soreness, Atherton was comforted to find that his toes were now doing better. He walked down the roadway, kicking up red dirt with an increasingly lighter step, and reflected on the compensations of jail. It would at least be a clean break with his drudgery, and if the term were not too long, a chance to begin again. His family would be summoned and he would see them daily. And if a white laborer was an oddity to be pampered, how much more so a white prisoner! Someone would come up with the money to bribe him a reasonably decent standard of living, maybe even something for his children's school fees. Someone would help him. Someone would take pity.

Atherton made the rise and curve that took him to the main street. At the sight of the Englishman, the Kamba officer, in shorts, Sam Browne belt, and white traffic gloves, dropped his hands. He peered into the sunlight, then, breaking into a large smile, waved once at the white man and returned to his mystical, ignored signing at the trucks.

Atherton stopped in his tracks, motionless, until a careering Land Rover drove him to the wooden sidewalk. He looked again at the policeman, clearly oblivious, then hurried down the walkway to Bimji's. The shop doors he passed were half open, half closed, the watchmen gone or just leaving, their *jikos* white ash. In Bimji's door, Guantai stood leaning on his staff and smoking a thin cigarette. His eyes were bloodshot and tired. At the Englishman's appearance he nodded, and walked away.

Atherton looked at the smashed crystal of his new watch and strode into the store. He could hear the Asian's voice from the back room, a complaint. On reflex, he walked into the office and stared at the intact window-pane above Bimji's desk.

"You want something?" The shopkeeper remained seated, peering down through the rimless glasses he wore only for doing accounts.

"No. Yes. I'd like . . . I want . . . a beer."

"Now? At mid-morning?"

"I'm thirsty."

"Very well." Bimji nodded to the cooler that stood by the shop doorway. Atherton retrieved a Tusker from the pool of lukewarm water in the case and opened it.

"The money, please."

Atherton froze, then fished a ten-shilling note from his pocket and threw it on the yellow desk. The Asian folded it once, then stopped. For the first time since he had entered the room, he looked at the Englishman's face.

"A bad night, Mr. Atherton?"—he forced a smile—"I know how it is. Not that I drink, but I do understand. Just get to work on time, please." The Asian pocketed the folded note and returned to his numbers.

# Kenya, 1980

Atherton held tight to his beer bottle and backed out the door. He ran to the front, whirling around as if he were being chased, and stumbled to the grassy alley by the store's side. They hadn't told Bimji. They hadn't told anybody. The bastards were not going to let anything change. There was not going to be any prison or wives cooking for him or money or punishment. Nothing was going to be different. Their equanimity was like a bloody tank plowing through the jungle. Nothing was going to change.

He smashed the bottle and sought to calm his trembling hands. A ragged line of dried blood ran along the tips of his fingers where they had pressed in vain against the edge of the Asian's cash box. Atherton wrapped his hands underneath his armpits, tight against himself, like a man chilled to the bone. Then he rose and walked to the Land Rover parked in front of Bimji's store. He climbed to the back and picked up a sack of beans, two hundred pounds of dried lentils, and swinging it to his shoulder, bowed his bruised back against the sun.

# Mexico, 2004

## A Second Language

Benson decided to study Spanish because after forty years it didn't seem to him that he had gotten that far with English. He returned to the south of Mexico, where two decades before he had gone with his first, his only, wife. He had set enough money aside to last for one month, including the Spanish lessons, if he stayed somewhere modest.

He looked for a small hotel on the Internet and found one in Oaxaca with its own website and goose. The goose was called Andrés and it danced—a simple animation, three images, a step, a bow, a turn of the head—above the room rates, a picture of the court-yard, and a view of the mountains from a rooftop pa-tio with azure walls and extravagant greenery.

Reassuringly, the Casa Reynaldo was also men-tioned in the guidebooks. The rooms were said to be clean and comfortable, Reynaldo was a real person—the owner—and reviewed as genial, and Andrés was a real goose who would play with children. Benson wrote Reynaldo an e-mail in Spanish, unavoidably without accents, given his shareware program, and reserved a room. He apologized for his grammar.

Soon he sat in the courtyard, eating oatmeal and papaya. The trees, cloaked in vines, stretched above the rooftop and rustled, from halfway up, in the breeze. The sunlight dappled the tabletop and the milk jug and the faces of the contented English couple across from him, who came from Uxbridge, or Oak's Bridge, and were travelling around the world, although the Pacific was going to be extremely hard to negotiate on a limited budget. The patches of light moved with the leaves and the wind and wandered over the couple's faces, darkening a cheek, then an eye, then half a nose, as if the two were spaniels auditioning coloration.

Benson listened intently—somewhere, in Peru, in Ecuador, there were still steamships, and propeller-driven planes that were old, but cheap—but, as the sun moved over his shoulders, its touch was too warm, the bougainvillea too purple, the strange little spiky flowers, whatever they were, too yellow for him to focus. Somewhere behind his chair, across the cobbled street, probably next to the demure, for Mexico, suburban church he had seen on each walk to the *zócalo*, a cock crowed. Roosters were crowing at all hours of day and night, an endless supply of false and redundant dawns. He had barely slept his first two nights, and then, on the third, only succeeded by melding the rucurucucus into his dreams. Look! They were saying, there is a tree growing atop each church tower. The sidewalks are littered with vanilla beans. Everywhere there is something remarkable.

The English couple bubbled on, dazed by their bravery at leaving everything behind. Benson nodded and plucked at his papaya. The bell at the gate rang and Reynaldo's ten-year-old son opened it. More sunlight poured in, nibbling the silhouettes of two women. The taller one juggled a backpack and a sparkling metal suitcase of the kind his father had travelled with in the fifties, made to withstand attacks and pressure and clumsiness, and held the smaller, older woman's hand. They stepped forward into the courtyard and three dimensions—the younger woman, with worry in her eyes, elegant in a billowy black dress, the older wearing an ancient *huipil*, embroidered in faded parrot colors, over khaki trousers—then vanished into Reynaldo's room with the desk and the big keys and the postcards of the ruins of Monte Albán. Feathers brushed Benson's leg. Another rooster crowed, right underneath his table.

The school of Spanish for those who did not speak it was a single-story building of cream stucco, already falling apart from the climate or the Richter seven-point-several that had shaken the valley in 1999. The cracks webbed out over the front, but the lines were neatly patched with a plaster painted a turquoise of heartbreaking purity. Everything seemed under control. Inside, the school's director determined with a twelve-question interrogation—How did you come here? Where will you go? Do the ruins of ancient civilizations please you?—that Benson was sufficiently far along for a private tutor. This pleased Benson, because despite a natural modesty, he was reluctant to try to speak Spanish in a group of the equally inept. That was, in fact, how he had often felt when conversing in his own language, as if in a roomful of wounded talk. But he was dismayed when the tutor emerged from a back room as a clearly North American man in his forties named Otto, with hair dyed a Leslie Howard yellow and a gleam of sweat at his lips.

They sat at a formica table in the school's front room.

"I have traveled everywhere," Otto told Benson, in what sounded to Benson like defensive but nevertheless authentically accented Spanish. The tutor waved a frayed cuff of his long-sleeved white shirt toward the mountains and the hard-to-navigate Pacific that lay beyond the barred window, "and I have learned much. But speak of yourself," he said, gazing hangdog into Benson's eyes.

Benson told Otto what he had eaten the day before and on what streets the restaurants were located. He then suggested, though from the look on his tutor's face, he might have commanded, that they take a walk. They both donned sunglasses and stepped back through the front door into the splendid light and heat of mid-morning.

As they walked, Benson pointed at whatever things

occurred to him—dwarf cacti under nets on the side-walk; sugar-cane skeletons in the shops; the machines, which looked like farm well pumps, used to grind nuts and twigs into chocolate—and Otto, after instants of what seemed, cyclically, distraction or thought or pan-ic, would supply their names. Then Benson formed questions around the names, diligently cloaking his bursts of curiosity in the grammar from his textbook.

"Why, a cactus, does it need for itself protection with a net?" he asked.

Otto swung his head from side to side. At the middle of its arc it dipped low enough so that Benson could see, over Otto's sunglasses, the tutor's lids flickering. "I don't know. Perhaps they have," Benson thought the word he heard was "enemies."

Benson racked his brains to conceive of a suitable enemy for a cactus. He wanted to ask if there were rac-coons in Oaxaca, but he didn't know how to say rac-coon. Instead, he asked "Do rats eat cactus?" correctly using a reflexive construction of the passive voice, which was optional under the circumstances, but el-egant, and which pleased him immensely, although even before Otto shrugged in response, Benson re-alized that any rat that could eat a cactus could eat through a net.

"Birds, I think." Otto waved his arm in that way he had—a scarecrow flopping a straw-filled limb—to in-dicate a whole sad world aswarm with aggressive fly-ing things.

Benson lifted his eyes to the park canopy above him where clouds of sparrow-like creatures settled then fled, from jacaranda to jacaranda, in a rainshower beating of wings. "Do you know what they're called?"

Otto shook his head. "*Ni una jota*," he said. Not a jot. The tutor looked down at his hands. He extended his fingers, held them out for an instant in the gesture of a magician, then pulled a flask from the pocket of his trousers. He offered it to Benson, which the younger man—Benson felt sure he must be younger—offended, declined. The teacher and student sat on the bench and watched the birds infiltrate the maze of topiary, each of the nameless creatures devouring a wealth of tiny berries the color of blood.

At the Casa Reynaldo, the tall woman who had checked in during breakfast sat beside him at the table for luncheon. Reynaldo's granddaughter brought them plates of spaghetti with a thin red sauce.

"You're American?" he asked.

"Very," she said.

"And the woman you're traveling with is . . . ?"

"My mother." She said it with some finality. "She knows all about Mexico." The woman paused, the fork halfway to her mouth. "I mean, she wrote a book, *All About Mexico*. In 1938, for Americans who were interested in the Revolution. You know, Cárdenas. Land for the poor. Folk-dancing? But she hasn't been back since they shot the students." The woman saw Benson's ping of confusion. "In 1968, before the Olympics. But things are better now, she thinks. So she tells me. I've never been here before."

The tall woman stopped to chew. "This is very good," she said, still munching. "But there's hardly any sauce and it's not at all spicy. Isn't that"—she leaned forward and wiggled her fingers—"uncharacteristic? Non-Mexican?"

Benson was happy with a chance to be knowledge-able for a woman he thought beautiful. He studied her dark, soft hair, the green eyes with the creases of his own age at their corners when she smiled. "It's a *sopa seca*. They call a course like that a 'dry soup.' Rice, too."

"Is that a joke?"

"No, it's just a different view of soup."

The green-eyed woman considered this, then con-tinued on her own track. "Because sometimes their names for food are jokes. In Mexico City my moth-er and I had *manchamanteles*, 'tablecloth stainer,' all these drippy fruits and juicy meats in a stew? It was wonderful. You hardly knew where you ended and it started." The woman rested her chin on her hands and gazed out in remembered contentment. "And then in English there's 'hot dog.' If that's not a joke, what is it?" Suddenly, it seemed to Benson almost angrily, she pushed her plate away from her and poured herself a cup of coffee from the covered enamel pitcher that stood on the table's corner closest to the kitchen.

"My mother is forgetting things now. Pretty much

everything, in fact. She wanted to come back here because she was forgetting"—the woman pursed her lips and outlined the words—"all about Mexico."

"Does she eat?" Benson immediately felt a flush of embarrassment and floundered to recover. "I mean, in public?" he said, though this was worse yet. She had just told him about the dinner in Mexico City. He had come to Mexico, in part, for exactly this reason, that the sentences in his own language were finishing more badly as he got older, his words throwing out wildly inappropriate threads leading to unintended locations. He scanned the woman's face for offense taken, but saw only her own understandably self-absorbed anxiety.

In a flush, Benson felt an overwhelming wave of sympathy. His own parents had both died in the prime of life—if such a thing were possible—but Alzheimer's, the blank plague! He had a friend at home whose father was the only banker in a small Iowa farm town. He had all the records strewn about his office yet he remembered nothing. No one in the town knew who owed whom what. Principal, interest, mortgages, responsibility—all were torn to strips in the brain's shredder, a bank president's jubilee-year socialism of precisely located memory loss. The townspeople would call the child in Des Moines when the parent went missing, and the son would find his father miles from the bank, asleep in a cornfield, healthy as a horse, his mind vacant, barely remembering the laces on his shoes.

"In the room. She'd rather."

# A Second Language

"I'm sorry."

"Don't misunderstand me. She's not, you know, a vegetable, or anything. She just likes to eat by herself. She nearly always has. I'll bring her something." The woman searched the table for a sugar bowl, and quickly added four spoonfuls to her coffee. "I'm sorry. A bad habit." Then she placed the spoon carefully down beside her cup and extended her hand. "I'm Maria. The Mexican influence."

Benson stood up, his hand holding hers. "Albert," he said, "the Swiss influence," then sat down again, mortified as he had been all his life at the garbled forms sexual attraction took in him. Beneath his shirt, the flush from his face spread to his shoulders.

"I'm a teacher." Both her hands now cradled her cup. "I teach history in Maryland."

"So do I." Benson gave a laugh that to him sounded unhinged, but that he sensed was emerging into the world as the pleasant chuckle of a man who has escaped the bonds of any consequence to his actions. Whatever he said now was going to be the sheerest fabrication. "I mean not history in Maryland. I teach Business English. At a community college. To foreign people."

"Business English?"

"Yeah, there are things you don't need to say, when you have a specific goal. In business." Benson stared straight ahead, avoiding her eyes. "And there are things—and words—that you need. You don't need to say, I mean you don't need to know how to say, for example,

'I remember the first summer of peacetime,' but you need to say, 'We can come to terms'—which by the words alone, if you don't know much English, makes absolutely no sense at all." Benson put his hands to his face and pressed his fingertips against his lids, astounded.

"I gouge, you gouge, we gouge?"

"Well, maybe. It's more functional English as opposed to imaginative English. 'Gouge' is sort of in the middle. Emotional English." The woman was looking at him, he thought, not unkindly. He smiled back winningly, he hoped.

Two blocks down from the Casa Reynaldo was a postage-stamp park. Set in a notch, before a yellow wall, under a yellow tree, there was a small statue of a short man in a waistcoat and tails. The birds, whom Benson had started to think of as the cactivores, puddled at the statue's base, pecking at unseen grain. He leaned to the worn bronze of the nameplate.

*Ingeniero Hernando Elote*, it read.

Benson stood back. Engineer Herman Corn. It seemed to him an odd name for a person, at least a Spanish or Mexican person. Not that there weren't Corns in America or England. Or Cornwall, certainly. Kornfelds, which was clearly cornfields, or Kerns. Was Kern corn? Old words flowed in his mind. *You are the promised breath of springtime that trembles on the brink of a lovely star.* Or was it *a kiss of springtime, a lonely star*? And was there something in between?

# A Second Language

Benson sat down on the wrought-iron bench, pulled his straw hat over his face and began, since he was in a foreign country with no one looking over his shoulder or making judgments or, if they were making judgments, they were probably just classifying him as an inexplicable foreigner, to hum the song softly, the way he remembered it.

One week in, it occurred to him that he hadn't seen the goose. He asked the woman who he assumed was Reynaldo's wife, Margarita (a new annex of rooms was sublabelled the Fonda Margarita), about the bird from the website, about Andrés.

Margarita—if that were who she was—ran a hand through her thick black hair and smiled broadly. "He is dead. But he is *disecado*."

"*Disecado*?"

"Yes, he is *disecado* in the back." She pointed behind the mahogany portal that led from the reception area to an inner office.

Benson didn't have a clue as to what *disecado* meant, although to Margarita the word seemed delightful as a rainbow. Why did this keep happening? To understand nearly everything should count for something, should be something, but it was to understand nothing if one linguistic black hole remained. Benson felt as if he were constantly looking up to see his whole sky of meaning sucked into such emptiness.

"But we are getting a new goose soon. Come tomorrow and I will show you." Then, although Benson had not shown the slightest motion of leaving, she waved a small goodbye.

Benson turned. Reentering the courtyard, he circled the twin cages where Miguel and Portero, two brilliant, eternally whistling parrots, lived. Then, in the corner, past the Caribbean-blue jeroboams of purified water and the barrel where they put the table-soiled napkins, he walked up the stairs to the balcony. Why, he wondered, was climbing a public staircase a joyous adventure here, but at home nothing? Benson suddenly remembered his Midwestern high-school stairwell, the fear and the completely unadventurous certainty of what he'd find, bigger older kids coming ceaselessly down, an insect horde.

But here, without effort, in what had become second nature in only a few days, yet without losing the conscious and exotic pulse of ritual, he could mount the narrow concrete steps, sun-warmed even through the foliage, push through the vines that coated the side wall, and reaching the top, cross the small enshrubbed patio on the office roof—with its generous Mesoamerican view stretching even to the lopped-off hilltop where the Zapotecs, themselves conscious of the grave pleasures of mounting steps, had built their pyramids—and let himself into his room. He hunted for his dictionary, which was under something or gone—Reynaldo's daughters cleaned pitilessly—and grabbed a pen from his suitcase. In his notebook of

Spanish, he wrote down the single mysterious word, *disecado*. Then Benson added in English the words he had understood. In the back. *Disecado* in the back.

"Stuffed."

Otto broke his Spanish-only rule. This was clearly something he could not mime. Then he reverted to Castilian. "Like a fish in a bar. Or a deer," the tutor put his hands on either side of his sad Baroque face—the face, Benson thought, of a saint being tormented under layers of dark paint—and crooked his fingers arthritically, "on the wall of a hunter."

Andrés was stuffed. In the back, forever. The mystery was solved. Tomorrow there would be a new goose.

"*La taxidermia*," added Otto after the fact, realizing late that there had been a simpler way out all along. "Now," he said, slowly pushing himself up from the formica table, "we go outside?"

In the market, in the butchers' quadrant, the whole under a vast corrugated roof, Benson navigated through the sectioned hogs and the tripe barrels. Watered-down blood pooled in the plastic tarps that underlay the tables. Cathedrals of dirty ice tumbled about him, with faint emissions of steam. The smells, real and imagined, of animal sweat twisting in the air made Benson feel as if he were trapped in a locker room, stripping down with a hundred head of cattle. He peered for reassurance down the long corridor of meat, to the sunlight of the street entrance where he could just see Otto, leaning against a brick pillar, pulling on a cigarette.

"I don't go inside," Otto had told him. "But you can come out to me with questions. It is not far, though you can be lost." *Perdido*, he had said, like Sarah Vaughan, though with more despair.

"You have agoraphobia?" Benson had asked, not unsympathetically. Remembering *taxidermia*, he plopped the Greek in more or less whole, but took a stab with one of the little tics of accentuation that seemed to work to let words like *béisbol* and *fútbol* get by. He wondered if one could be agoraphobic—in English? in Spanish?—about an indoor as well as an outdoor marketplace.

"*Un poquito*." A small little. The tutor spoke the words with such intense sadness that Benson half expected to be handed a ball of twine, so as not to lose himself in the labyrinth.

"Well then, I'll come back. Whenever I need help." Benson looked for a response, but got none. He turned to walk into the dark gauntlet of stalls.

"It's all the buying and the selling," Otto had said, with that same flamenco sadness, and waved his scarecrow wave.

Now back among the dead animals, Benson looked to the outer rim of the market where everything sold was Chinese: sacks of fat plastic twine and, to stuff in them, shirts, pants, and hose, shiny and synthetic, all woven of hard-edged distinct threads. Taut Indian faces poked out in the midst of t-shirts, of red and aquamarine dresses.

He saw Maria and her mother, tall and short, trolling through the cloth like Don Quixote and Sancho Panza, and he waded toward them, stepping on the sheen of blood and water, meeting where the fish blended to textiles.

Maria seemed to smile brightly at seeing him, and left her mother, gabbling fluently amid piles of soft cloth, a few paces behind.

"She eats this stuff up, loves it. She won't speak to anyone new in English, but every time she says something in Spanish, it's an accomplishment. She remembers the words. Do you want to walk?" Not waiting for an answer, Maria leaned toward her mother across the sea of fabrics, miming above the noise, then stepped back to Benson and took his arm.

"She says it's all right."

"In Spanish?"

"Yes, actually. She absolutely adores markets, always has."

"I'd think it would make her uneasy, with all the confusion." Benson stopped, unsure which aisle to make for, then headed for a row of stalls stacked high with mezcal bottles.

"You just don't like chaos. For Mom, this isn't all that different from regular life. She likes accumulation, and in a market, you always go out with more stuff than you had coming in. It makes her feel good. How do you choose?" She gestured toward the shelves of bottles—a multitude of ambers—both with and without worms.

Benson, in his most recent Spanish, selected one with a distinctive label, twelve years old, dark amber, *con gusano*. A worm curled like a dry leaf at the bottom. "It's really only a caterpillar, you know. It's just the same word."

"I do know. Why is that better?"

Benson had never asked himself the question. "I think because worms live in the dirt and caterpillars move on top of it." He handed the bottle to Maria to consider the creature. "Is there a right answer?"

"Not really." She turned it in her hands. "Of course, caterpillars become butterflies."

"Moths, I think, in this case."

"Same difference. And worms don't. Caterpillars are only temporarily worms. They're not locked into it. That, on the other hand, is decidedly untemporary." She pointed toward an outcrop of the butchers' section on their left, where a row of pig's heads on spikes reared above a bed of bloody ice. "They used to do that to the heads of traitors along London Bridge. A reminder to us all."

Maria suddenly returned the mezcal bottle to Benson and spun him toward the southeast and the candy quadrant. Again she mimed her intentions to her mother, now twenty yards behind them, still happily talking to Indians amidst the cloth. Benson could feel her hand on his back, pushing. "Now," she said, "I think you need chocolate."

Two weeks in, Benson awoke near midnight with the certainty, unverified by anything except inner panic, that he was running out of money. From the bottom of his toilet kit he scrabbled behind the toothpaste, removed the thinned sheaf of cash and his hologrammed bank card, and went out looking for an ATM.

There was always so much new magic. Twenty years before, every bank transaction had been an effortful dance of documents: travelers' cheques, passports, tourist cards, receipts; the thumping of murky purple stamps, the shuffling of inky fingers, a line for the paperwork, a window for the cash. Now under the blackness so different from home—the stars with their separate colors—the chiclet sellers sat on the sidewalk before Cirrus and Plus logos, the ATMs humming softly behind. Still, as he stood in the arcade cubicle at the edge of the *zócalo*, he couldn't get his account balance, but only a heap of Mexican notes and a profound sense of poverty.

False poverty, of course, Benson told himself, stuffing the new money into his pocket. His poverty was nothing compared with that of the chiclet seller, a woman with a black band of cloth across her forehead who sat impassively, unpassably, on a low stool in the middle of the doorway, her wild-haired child twirling in orbit around the spread folds of her skirt. Between the boxes of pink candy and the careening infant, it was impossible to get cash without an invoice of guilt. Nevertheless, he had, what—a week's? ten days' worth?—of bed, board, and Otto's fees before he would have to return to the blank slate of home.

"Do you have a cheaper room?" he asked Reynaldo.

The owner did. It was darker and smaller than the first, but it had the same crushed twist of dried flowers nailed to the wall above the head of the bed, the same beleaguered pine dresser, assembled in haste. There was no window, so the only fresh air swirled in above the transom of the door, cool at night, sure to be almost poisonous by day. Benson found it snug and unthreatening, though after a few minutes, mixed with time and the outside darkness, a little threatening. The lower ceiling, the walls closing in, his money running out.

Benson smoothed the lace doily on top of the dresser and carefully put down on it the box of chocolate and the bottle of mezcal he had bought at the market. He paused a minute, considering the still life, then, retrieving the thick warm glass from the washbasin, he poured himself an inch of the liquor.

As he poured, the pickled, shriveled caterpillar slid slowly from one side of the bottle to the other, like the snow in a souvenir dome. Benson broke off a rough piece of the chocolate and placed it in his mouth. The taste cheered him. This was the real thing, he thought. *México auténtico*! These people had invented the substance. It tasted substantial, the cocoa and the sugar in separable, grainy lumps he could roll over his tongue—first a puff of bitterness and caffeine, then a sweet blow of honey. He washed the chocolate down with the mezcal, its warm flush followed by the soft explosion of something planty, damp, and green, a lotus pod crushing in his mouth. A Hindu fable he had once read of had told of a man cupping water from the ocean. I remove abundance from abundance and still abundance remains, the man, standing in the shallows, had said. Who did he think he was talking to, Benson had always wondered, jealous as if of a perfect lover at the man's obvious satisfaction.

Later, the two thin blankets pulled about his shoulders, Benson heard, in among the birds and the wind's sigh, slapping sounds rising through the floorboards from the room below that Maria shared with her mother. A whistle, a *thwap*, a rush of breath. Another *thwap*.

"Solitaire," Maria said, alone again in the bright light of breakfast, but seemingly happy to talk. "She plays concentration when she can't sleep. The doctor recommended memory games. Personally, I think exercise is a crock. It's not as if the brain is a muscle, is it? It's like trying to run faster by thinking very hard. The doctor thought it would help, but I think it's just training her for disappointment."

Maria put her hand on Benson's arm. "What do you think?"

"I can't imagine," Benson spoke slowly, barely able to think for the touch, "what it's like to have to work at remembering." He looked down at her hand, still warm on his skin. Should he cover it with his own? "I don't mean that. I mean, we only work at finding the things we've already remembered. We work to re-call things, to pick up things we've put down in our memory, and sometimes we can't find them. But, if we're healthy, we don't have to work at putting things down in the first place. That just happens, doesn't it?" And what was *remember* anyway, Benson thought, still swirling at Maria's touch, the mere word itself? The opposite of *dismember,* the reattachment of lost limbs? "Things just go down, like gravity."

"But that's great!" Before he had done anything to respond, Benson realized, Maria lifted her hand, to gesture it seemed, but maybe this was all of it, maybe all she had wanted was his unintentional or at least only partially understood encouragement. "If you can practice it, concentration would be perfect. A cross-word puzzle would just be what you call recall, *dah-da, dahda,*"—Maria, cheered, beat the rhythm with a spoon—"but concentration, holding on to the image of that card you just turned over, that would really be remembering, putting something down in the first place. That's great."

Benson felt happy to give her hope, if that was what he had done, although he wished he knew more exact-ly how he had done it. How could one practice gravity?

# A Second Language

She smiled warmly at him, as warm as her hand had been, and the lines at the corners of her eyes, which so reassured him of their joint passage through time, were etched more sharply and invitingly in the sparkling sunlight, in spite of any mutual misunderstanding.

In Benson's dreams, amid the crowing, Johnny Mathis sat on a folding chair before a table of multicolored toys: armadillos, macaws, jaguars, all small as beetles and painted in red and yellow stripes, and white dots, and green zigzags, each with a dangling, spring-sprung head that nodded with the breeze. And as he held them up to Benson on his palm, he sang. *Maria! Maria! Maria!* The most beautiful sound he ever heard. All the beautiful sounds in the world from a single bird! *Maria! Maria! Maria!* And the little animals all waved along their loose heads to the tune and the wind so enchantingly that Benson bought them all, flinging colorful peso notes on the table and scooping up the toys until they spilled from his pockets like grain, like gold. Benson tried to pick up the fallen ones, but as quickly as he could gather them from the ground, new ones fell from his pockets, and Johnny Mathis, smiling, singing, misunderstanding Benson's frantic scooping, replenished the supply so that Benson could barely stand in the heap he was becoming of cheerful little toys.

He saw a concert advertised in a gallery—a banner

held in the hands of papier-maché skeleton in mariachi dress—and decided to ask her to go with him. That she seemed eager to go nearly overjoyed him and, as they walked at twilight toward the *zócalo,* Benson found it easy to talk with her. He felt he could say anything he wanted: how much he liked tropical vegetables or running his hand lightly along the walls by the sidewalk in the soft night air, feeling the dry chalky film of dust on the bump of stucco; how much he enjoyed the idea of building new things from old ones, like the church next to the ruins of Mitla fashioned from the stone brickwork of the old tombs.

Though when he said that, Maria gave him a searching, disapproving look. "Oh, good. Right on. Rip up their temples to make the foundation of your church." She pulled closer about her neck the long nubbly cotton scarf that she was wearing with the gravity of a vestment. "Destructive triumphalism. It's the curse of the world."

"I didn't mean it that way." Benson put his hands in his pockets. How *did* he mean it? And what was triumphalism? "I meant it more cozy—cozy and thrifty. Like barn boards, you know, paneling a room with barn boards? It's not just wasting stuff or letting go. It's provident, and conserving. And imaginative, if they're in decent shape."

"That's like saying making mortar from the blood of slaves is thrifty. They're dead anyway. What else are you going to do with the blood?"

# A Second Language

Benson shrugged and looked down at the sidewalk, at first only in a reflexive effort to look appealingly contrite. This was, though it had been years and he hadn't quite thought of it so plainly until now, a date. If he couldn't be smart, Benson reasoned, his categories rapidly being sucked back into adolescence, he could at least, however ludicrous it was for a man of middle age, be cute. Or abashed, though he had never been certain exactly what that—any more than triumphalism—was, but what this seemed to call for was abashed. But then he sprang to his own defense, because, in fact, he did genuinely feel contrite or, at least, inadequate.

"I don't really disagree with you. I was just thinking something more . . . ," Benson waved his arm, in what he sensed chillingly was Otto's gesture, ". . . down to the ground. I think you're more of a big-picture person than I am."

It was true, he thought. He was short-term, not that he didn't think about history. Going to Mexico without thinking about history was like going to San Diego. But he didn't have the long view that Maria obviously had. He, too, saw the crumbled stones and the shattered pyramids. Though when he had taken the short bus ride up to Monte Albán, they didn't seem quite so shattered as he had remembered from the time he had gone with his wife, twenty years before. Men in white jackets were fixing the pyramids now. He'd seen them puttering around with wheelbarrows and trowels, putting in clean and fresh-cut stones.

But that was just it. He tried to fly over history, take the long view, but he was like one of those birds in the *zócalo* that neither he nor Otto knew the names of. He tried to stay aloft, but he kept landing on a fact he liked—the men with the trowels, a single white stone, the dampness in the air—and then flitting away to another attractive fact, unaware of what had gone before or came after, the whole idea of sequence and consequence gone completely distraught as he pursued whatever facts grabbed him by the senses. The nameless birds did it as a flock, moving like starlings—except they were smaller, lighter, more graceful than starlings—but the more Benson did it, over the minutes and the years, the more he realized that there was no longer a flock beside him. The others had gathered their berries. They had eaten and moved on, while he swooped and rose and turned by himself, alone.

They curved around the Templo de Santo Domingo and left the cement of the sidewalk, their shoes crunching the even gravel of the path that bordered the church, the moonlight catching the edges of the smoothly raked scallops, the soft waves of fine stones.

"Was it just the Spaniards?" Benson felt compelled to pursue his earlier thought. "If you leave aside the good and bad of the deal—if you can do that—the pre-Columbians built things out of the skulls of sacrificial victims. And they ate the flesh. They drew pictures of limb bones in cooking pots in the codexes."

"Codices," Maria corrected, then apologized. "Sorry, I'm a historian. Professional reflex."

"No, that's OK. Thanks. Codices." He pronounced the word carefully; she was a nice person. "It was ritual, but it was protein, too, don't they think?"

"Cannibalism as recycling?"

Benson stood his ground with gravity. "I don't endorse cannibalism," he said, though as he spoke, he was unsure if he had real people in his mind—the ones here, now—or only the little clay figures in the museum dioramas, marching up and down the pyramids to bring gifts and have their hearts, bloodless and nearly unbreakable, torn out.

"Good. That's good." Maria's voice softened. "My husband and I once had a cat that used to do that."

"Cannibalism?" Benson was even more startled by the husband than by the cat.

"No, he, it was a he, would just leave the—what do you call them—remains?"

"Sounds good."

"The remains, the parts he didn't eat. He'd just leave them, but eventually they accumulated in the same spot, under a tree. A little funerary heap of vole skulls. The bugs got the soft parts. He wasn't making a point, of course. It was unintentional, but it was a cat's kind of building. I used to think he could visit it, look at the skulls, and maybe remember the hunts." She turned toward him. "I don't have him anymore, by the way. My husband, that is. The cat has passed on as well."

She moved closer to him, and Benson could hear the light, wind-like sound of her legs walking in the smooth cloth of her dress. He leaned toward her, trying to be companionable, to match her steps on the descent, twilit and gradual, into the light and music of the downtown streets, but he could see Maria thinking, sure that she was absorbed either in her husband, whoever he might be, or in the cruel, elaborate civilization domestic cats would establish, if left to their own inclinations.

And what was he thinking himself? Benson wasn't sure he was thinking anything he could call his own. Certainly he was waiting to be helpful, waiting for her to supply him with something he could consider and respond to, but was that what she wanted, what any human being wanted of another? He blamed himself for being caught up too much in the moment, yet he didn't know what to do instead. Without memory and with only the faintest expectation, he was only a sympathetic ear, savage and detached. The thought frightened him.

The concert was terrible, though the setting was lovely. They sat on wooden chairs put out in the courtyard of an institution of education, and listened, surrounded by elegant archways and obscure corridors, to a Bach quartet played by a violin, two oboes, a cello, and a supernumerary snare drum. The drummer, a seemingly starving man with a squared black beard and a feral, intense expression, explained his choice of instruments at tedious length, gesturing with his brushes. Benson had little formal knowledge of music, but bad intonation could cause him genuine pain. The unmatched oboes, the sad sighs of the strings, and the leader, whisking steadily on his drum under a rectangle of stars, carried Benson against his will to a strange and uncomfortable place. Two days earlier he had nearly been struck in the street by a pickup filled with dishwashers and an ornately painted sign on the rear panel that read *Solo dios maneja este camión*—only God is driving this truck—though, in fact, a large straw Stetson with huge hands seemed to be at the wheel. Sitting in the severe chair in the growing chill of the Mexican night, Benson listened to the sprung Bach and the sensation of the truck swerving toward him formed again in his mind, both threats joining together in a stream of roaring apprehension, though, next to him, Maria sat sleeping in her chair.

"I'm sorry I was so tired," she said later, walking back through the streets, the soft trees.

"You didn't miss anything."

"I know. It's just that each day is hard."

"I can imagine," Benson said, though as he said it, he doubted he could.

Outside her door—her and her mother's door, the yellow light flickering through the uneven transom pane—Maria gently kissed his cheek and said goodnight. Benson walked past the parrots and up the enchanted stairway, past the room that had been his the week before, to the lower-rent alcove around the corner.

Seated on the narrow bed, he blamed himself for not being complex enough, even after all his living, for a woman like Maria. She was preoccupied—justifiably, understandably—with forgetting, and he, it seemed to him, had forgotten too much of his own life even to be a distraction, less still a gift, to someone of her burdens.

In the middle of the night, at another cock's crow, Benson awoke with a start and remembered in its entirety what he had completely forgotten: a small crafts market for tourists, blocks south of the central building of stalls, that he and his wife had seized on during their honeymoon walk through the city, smelling the new paint of the entrance sign, the fresh whitewash on the outer walls.

It was a roofless open yard without shelter, an attempt to recreate a village plaza and nothing to do with the real warren of things up toward the *zócalo.* "All that buying and selling," Otto had said. But here there were just straw mats laid out over cement polished the green of grass and on them rows of new-shined pots, glazed a darker green and black, like stones in a stream.

The small stalls were only half-filled and, though it was meant to mimic a mountain village plaza, it had the smell of a suburban development—more plats than houses, more speculation than grass. Everywhere

# A Second Language

about it was the newly constructed odor of hopeful geometry. The vendors wore their newest clothes, and a priest, a windbreaker over his shirt and collar to obey the law against clerical garb in public, walked through them, sprinkling holy water on their commercial expectations. His manner was mournful and cramped, his eyebrows heavy and singed with an ashen gray that matched his eyes. Beside him a boy swung a censer, the smoke spiraling furious in the strong warm wind, and just behind came three mariachis in full finery as vividly out of tune in Benson's memory as last night's Bach. Benson, his wife, and the other tourists fell in behind, a procession in tiny steps.

The priest's Spanish was unintelligible or perhaps not Spanish at all, but an Indian tongue. Zapotec. Nahuatl. Twenty years later, even with a dictionary and guide book on the night table, Benson was still stymied by the names, the effort like reading cue cards from a distant past. For whatever reason—the language, the strain of the battered trumpet and guitarrons, the entrancement of the motion itself, small measured steps among the pots—Benson could barely discern whether the priest was marking birth or death, the sprinkled water baptismal or funereal, Christian or pagan, European or American.

But now, in his dream and his waking, in this night and that day, everything was suffused with an intense sweetness. He knew a joy of recollection, not called for or labored at, that he had once loved a woman in a way that had spilled over into a love for every object that he saw and remembered, every sweet uncomplicated toy, every sweetly curved pot—fire-black underneath, a splash of shiny green glaze above—that lay before him. And he remembered not just one pot, but row upon row of them spread on the blankets, all slightly different, not in their shape or purpose, but in the splashes of green glaze that curled around them, as varied as sea waves or leaves or the longings of the heart.

Benson realized now that everything had been laid down then—everything, all the betrayals, incandescences, abrasions that now blurred in his mind into the long arc of love's decline—like objects placed in a time capsule and sealed within a cornerstone, to be dug up and revealed twenty years later. Then he had wanted, he remembered, to buy everything he saw.

In the end, though, they didn't buy anything, not knowing where to put the plates, the bowls, the pots, or what to put in them. Surely they were of use in Mexico, but at home he would not store grain or carry water from a well. At home they would just be empty, decorative, and accusing. He had taken nothing home but an unaccountable sense of beginning. Now he remembered it all: the wind, warm and powerful, scouring the marketplace; its touch on his skin, dry and restoring; the vision of hills beyond.

# East Africa, 1858

## The Immanence of God in the Tropics

Andrew Seavey's brow was unlined, his skin drawn tight across small features. He had a thin fine nose, hazel eyes, and lips without fullness. When Seavey sang hymns after morning reading, his mouth formed a small and perfect circle, a miniature of God's praise.

To the other missionaries he seemed incapable of throwing up. But, in fact, he had carried a bubble of nausea at the top of his stomach from Southampton to Gibraltar, all down the coast of Africa to the Cape. For a few hours in the pale green waters of Table Bay the sickness lifted, but at sea again, it returned. As a result Seavey had an air of expectancy about him; he had spent six weeks waiting patiently to be relieved of his distress. He ate little. Alone, in the safety of his cabin, he belched air.

The seasickness shriveled his sociability. Seavey spent the afternoons playing his flute on the afterdeck. He slept often and dreamt of heaving stones. The muscles of his body had grown flaccid in the inactivity of shipboard life; he felt himself disappearing. Though he tried to listen to the other missionaries, his attention was constantly shrinking back to the swallow in his throat and the uneasiness that floated at the nape of his neck. He was not willing to dispute church organization with Procter and the others. Questions of ritual and liturgy seemed pointless to him. But theology began to matter. He talked with Charles, one of the African Christians who had come aboard the *Lyra* at the Cape, dutiful men, orphans and freed slaves, who were to serve as interpreters with the savages of the interior.

"What color is God's skin?" Charles asked him.

Seavey thought a moment—satisfied with his responsibility—and said, "Well, of course, it is all colors: black, brown, yellow, and white. God has created the natural world—the sea, the earth, and the air—out of himself. He possesses all attributes, all colors."

"But," Charles asked, "he is more like some things than others, isn't it? He is not like everything. Aren't we created in his image?"

Seavey thought again. He considered the looking-glass hanging on his cabin wall. "Yes, Charles, we are an image of him, but an image is only a partial thing, a reflection of the whole. Look at this mirror. Do you see your image in it?"

Charles nodded. The black man studied his hair, the line of his nose. He ran a finger across the full skin of his lips.

"This is your image, but it is less than you. In this

image I can hold your head between the tips of my fingers; it is smaller than you. And it is flat. It has only the two dimensions of length and breadth. It is your image, but it has no roundness, no shape. As you yourself are more than your image, so God is more than us. We have only one color to our skins. God has all colors."

Seavey's talk seemed to satisfy Charles. The black man was full of curiosity about the civilization which he had adopted, but there was a threshold of strangeness, of sheer peculiarity, which he often approached, but once having sighted it, never crossed. It was not the technological power of the British that dazzled him so much as this magic barrier, the splendid irrationality of their thought. The African returned to his work.

But Seavey was disturbed. He had always thought of God as an abstract thing, a force rather like sunlight, strength without substance. But if he possessed all attributes, then God—as he had himself just told Charles—must be full of shapes. It was only *natural*— the word seemed particularly appropriate to Seavey— that he could appear out of whirlwinds, in pillars of fire and smoke. He was like a human but more so, more like those images the Hindus made than like any Christian painting: God was a thing with many arms and feet, with a breath of fire and smoke, with odors. Incense and sweat curled the missionary's nostrils. Seavey, rocking in his cabin in the humid night, became obsessed with the physical body of God.

"But you are wrong, Andrew," Procter told him. The sea was glassy now, calm, the water turquoise. Two birds broke the surface at a distance in twin dives, a wriggling of their tails, then reappeared with silver fish pinioned in their beaks. There was no sound from the sails. "God is the creator of the universe but he is not part of it. It is a thing separate from himself as a box made by a carpenter is not the same thing as the carpenter. To believe that God is physically equivalent to the natural world is a foreign idea." Procter mopped his brow. "I think it is Chinese."

"Oh no. I don't mean that he is equivalent. I just thought he might include the natural world, but still be something more." The birds reappeared, fishless, and shook the water from their backs. "Your carpenter, for instance, is only separate from his creation—his box—if you look at things in a materialistic way. Spiritually, the box and the carpenter are one, aren't they, if the box has been made with care and love? I mean, isn't it our souls that organize the random matter of the universe—the light and dust and elements—and hold them in the shape of our bodies? And if our souls are organizing principles—subsidiary of course to the Divine Principle which has, in its turn, organized them—then why can't the wood, paint, and nails of the box also be organized by our souls and be a part of us, as our bodies are a part of us?

"You see," continued Seavey with a note of pleading in his eyes that made Procter think, uncomfortably, of a golden retriever, "if spirit—God's as well as our own—is separate and distinct from the body of the world, then we, and God as well, live nowhere. We are ghosts, cut off from being. We have no substance. There is, quite exactly, nothing to us." Seavey ran a hand nervously through his thinning hair. "Doesn't that thought frighten you?"

Procter didn't know what to think about Seavey. Crawford, Simpson, and Jones, the Mission's other junior men, suggested there was perhaps too much free time on board ship and organized a more intensive program of study. In the mornings they read Dr. Livingstone's notes on the Tswana language. It was not the tongue that their own savages would speak, but it was no doubt related. Besides, the discipline of grammar was comforting. It protected them against the feeling of the ocean as the floppy hats of ship's canvas protected them against the sun and sky. The working sailors of the ship disdained such gear; instead they wore bandannas, soaking them in water on the hot days to cool their foreheads. As a consequence the faces of the ship's crew darkened while the missionaries' skin remained pale, unimprinted by the elements and the long voyage.

There was nothing yet for them to do. After so much preparation—the addresses from retired missionaries, courses in simple medicine, prospectuses of abridged catechisms—the idleness shipboard was a brutality. Each of the five men, upon his decision to take to another continent, had made an imagined sacrifice; they were relinquishing the company of their equals and the guidance of their betters for a life among lower, less complete people. Crawford had left a fiancée behind in Britain and Procter, a wife and child—dear ones they were not likely to see for years.

It was not the physical hardships they feared. Livingstone had assured them that the valley where he was sending them was, in fact, quite pleasant. It was more a fertile prairie than a jungle. There were woodlands that alternated with meadows and rich black bottomland by the streams. Farming it, the doctor told them, was so simple that even the Africans themselves had done it, tilling and harvesting in an organized, but barely conscious way, as bees made honey.

But the texture of life would inevitably be poorer, the social fabric woven all of straight lines of dominion and teaching. After all was said and done, they were to live among strangers who dressed in loincloths or less, who wore metal rings as big as horseshoes in their ears and plugs of brass through their nostrils and whose musical instruments had but a single string. "A tolerance for boredom," Livingstone had told them, "is the first requirement of a successful missionary. You must attend happily while they try to please you in a million poor ways. They will feed you sour milk and expect you to be delighted. They will give you a sick goat and expect praise. They will build you a house that leaks and a roof that is six inches too short for a white man's height. Your mind will swim with thoughts you cannot express in their language and you will spend the rest of your life talking down. Such complexity of thought as you can muster will come only in dreams. You will repeat anecdotes to each other as men in prison might and the conversations of your fellows will grow stale. Since the intimate watchfulness of family will be lacking to check you, you will be prone to delusions. You will grow to believe strange things."

It was starting, thought Procter, with Seavey and his overheated imagination. "I believe," Procter told him in a deliberate effort to calm the man, "that your theological doubts can be traced to simple disturbances of your own mind at the thought of leaving behind those you cherish. Do you come from a pleasant town?"

"Most pleasant."

"Well-peopled?"

"I don't understand you."

"Is there a crowd of people and many comings and goings? Small active farms and an energetic civil life? What I mean is, you've not lived in a wilderness."

"By no means. There is nothing wild about Hertfordshire."

"Well there you are," Procter warmed to his task. Thinking was such a simple thing when one came down to it. "You are leaving the city for wild country. At home your responsibilities were brought upon you without discussion. There was a mutual acceptance of what was expected. You knew it; the people in your care knew it. There was no need to think about it. But with your responsibilities so clearly defined, and sharply limited, there was little check upon your feelings. Your actions were so clearly hedged in that your feelings could safely wander, since they had no consequences. You could feel or imagine whatever you chose, since you were sure to behave properly.

"But in Africa, there will be no such check. We will have only ourselves to keep an eye on each other. Your imagination will have consequences. If you think something improper"—Procter leaned his bulk over Seavey; the man had a strong odor of sweat about him and behind was the smell of the sea, so that it seemed to Seavey a large creature, a seal or walrus, was cautioning him—"it may lead to improper action. The Africans may be misled.

"I don't mean to say that thought isn't dangerous even in England, but you are correctly aware that error will be infinitely more potent in Africa. You know that and are, no doubt, a little frightened. You believe a housecleaning of your thoughts is necessary."

At Seavey's feet a mouse skittered from under a pile of canvas and sniffed the resistant breeze. The missionary withdrew his face a few inches from Procter's and felt the wind cool his forehead. "That may all be so, Arnold. But just because you can account for my doubts, that doesn't mean they're not real. It's not you that has to live with them."

On the seventeenth of January, off the East African

coast, the island of Johanna appeared: a soft breast of land above the green translucent sea. The island was not at all African; rather, it was Arab. There were palm trees along the harbor and square, whitewashed buildings. The streets of the town were narrow and ran with foul water in the late afternoon storms. As on the ship, there were still no women to be seen. The thought disturbed Seavey. On the Lyra he had expected not to see females. But on land he expected women, as he expected the floor would no longer rock beneath him.

Upon landing, the party of missionaries was greeted by Consul Adams, the lone Briton on the island, a man with silver-white whiskers and an eyepatch he wore now on one eye, now on the other. "For the sun," he told Seavey. "Otherwise I'd spend all my time squinting." Adams appeared delighted to have the chance to exercise his office. He arranged the rental of a small house, owned by the Prince Abdallah, and planned a dinner for the group.

"Normally I do nothing but wait for a living. The native boats bring in the spices, which I weigh and grade and store until the company ship comes along." He smiled a smile—firm, comforting and wistful— that convinced Seavey the man must once have been the captain of a vessel. "But they come along only once every three months—twice on the way out to India and twice on the way back. The monsoon, you know."

"Of course," said Procter, who as Seavey had begun to notice, deeply disliked not knowing anything.

"What do you eat?" Seavey asked the consul.

"Eat? Why, everything. These fellows are the best gardeners in the world." He leaned over close to Seavey, his whiskers catching the sun. "Have you ever eaten a fresh mango? Or ham from a pig that's never had to shiver in his life?"

Seavey was shocked. He pulled forward the wicker chair on which he sat. "But I thought the Mohammedans didn't eat pork. "

"Not your normal-run islander. But Prince Abdallah lets me keep pigs for my own use. When he's with white men, he'll eat some himself. And drink, too. You'll see tonight. It's all by way of experiment, of course. The Prince is something of a philosopher. You see, he'll never be Sultan himself; that's for his brother. It gives Abdallah a certain freedom. He doesn't even like to use the title Prince. He says it shows too much pride."

Seavey settled into his room in Abdallah's house. It was a villa of whitewashed stucco perched above the waves on the eastern side of the island—the side that faced the open sea. From the window, a trim square sealed with a shutter of dark red wood, he could see the ocean and sky, twin endless bands of a lighter and darker blue. As he watched the play of sunlight on cloud taking shape across the heavens, the succession of images seemed to him a panorama of divine versatility, God throwing out a series of quick sketches in uncorrected strokes, the way the Japanese were said to paint in ink. Each effort was at once unfinished and perfect, the light and shadow full of implication as if the painter's thoughts were running ahead of his hand. The balance between the abstract and the concrete, the geometric and the sensual, delighted Seavey. He was pleased with his thoughts and the working of his mind. He folded his woolen trousers out of the sea trunk and laid his socks in rows upon the bed's soft cloth, happy to live in a world ruled so gracefully.

Adams had sent his men scurrying over the island to gather delicacies. The banquet that evening started with a salad of coconut palm for which an entire tree had been cut down and stripped to reach the heart of the top. The firm, moist flesh of the palm was layered with slices of a rosy-pink onion that tasted to Seavey peculiar and over-exuberant, like some strangely sweetened earth. Between courses, over glasses of an indefinable sherbet, the men compared their religions.

"We do not believe," said the Prince, "that any man or saint or god can stand between Allah and the believer. Thus it is not the divinity of your Christ which we would challenge—that may merely be excess enthusiasm—but the role that he plays in the story of the world. We respect Jesus, but I fear the Christ you make of him is an evasion of responsibility."

The Prince spoke excellent English. He also spoke French. Adams whispered to Seavey that the Arab, for all the firmness of his opinions, had an English Bible of which he was very fond and was said to cry over it.

"But your highness," Procter smiled broadly, rolling up his sleeves for the mental fight, "for those of our Church what you are calling the role of Jesus is revealed truth. It's as real as this table or tomorrow's sunrise. We don't choose our theology like a man before a buffet. Our truth is thrust upon us. "

"Actually, Arnold," interjected Seavey, "I find something appealing in a lack of intermediary between myself and God. Don't you?" He added the question, not from any real interest in Procter's opinion, but as a sop to the older missionary, whose irritation at being contradicted Seavey could sense, like a growing humidity in the wind.

"I wouldn't get too close to that idea if I were you, Seavey. It's a fire that's burned better men than you."

"Mr. Procter is quite right there," added the Prince. "They burned the saint Hallaj for no less. Though of course they first whipped him with a thousand strokes, cut off his limbs, hung him on a gibbet and then beheaded him." The Prince leaned back, recollected, and sighed. "I believe his last words were: 'alone with the Alone.' If we are vessels of the divine spirit"—Abdallah lifted the silver cup of water to his mouth; a fly fled his lips—"we must be careful not to shatter at the sound of Allah's voice. We must retain our shape."

"But perhaps the important thing is to listen. What we answer isn't crucial as long as we respond somehow. Don't you find that true, your highness, among your own people? I mean that some don't listen at all."

# The Immanence of God in the Tropics

"Just so. Only certain people hear, though all are . . . ," Abdallah paused and sought his word, ". . . addressed." The young Prince fidgeted in his chair. He was a small man with olive skin and black tight curls that fell around his temples. He seemed overwhelmed by the opulence of his clothes. "For myself, I cannot understand people not hearing. Slaves perhaps or people with too much work to do, but not men like ourselves."

At the mention of slaves, Seavey turned toward the serving women. They were all obviously African: their nostrils wide and flared, their lips thick, the skin of their cheeks a satin-black. They wore red sashes drawn tight around their waists, their breasts held in halters of thick white cotton. Only Adams saw Seavey's surprise. "What did you think they were, sir, gentlemen's daughters?" the old consul whispered to Seavey, then spooned the cooling syrup to his lips.

Seavey stumbled back to the thread of his thought. "Do you ever feel," he asked the young Prince, "that being close to God makes one feel distant from other men?"

"Do you?"

"I do. When I was home in England I felt that prayer was something one did with one's fellows. But lately, sometimes, the prayer of others obstructs me. I feel I should lock myself into a small room and pray alone. But then I don't pray exactly, so much as I just sit there. It's as if I didn't feel the need of prayer at that moment."

"Perhaps God is addressing you directly."

"It's not that big of a thing"—Seavey swung his

arms in the air, trying to represent the missing quality he could not otherwise describe. "It doesn't feel like revelation, so much as alertness."

"Dr. Livingstone told us," intruded Procter, "that a kind of irritability was the first sign of fever. He meant it, of course, in the scientific sense, as if you were prodding a one-celled creature under a microscope and it shrank back sharply from the needle."

"I never feel that way myself," mused the Prince.

Seavey felt he was making a terrible mistake, but he had to continue. "It's as if I were in a room filling up with a mist. At first it is sweet-smelling and it gives a new and pleasing quality to the light. But then this mist—this different air—expands and presses me. I find myself searching for breath, but I can no longer breathe."

"So you feel God is choking you?"

"Yes. Sometimes."

"This is not God. This is heat-stroke." Abdallah tilted his head, smiled, and smoothed the linen of his cloak. "If God really choked you, you'd be dead."

Seavey watched Procter's brow pursing in dismay. He saw the curiosity in Adams' eyes. The consul was looking at him as if Seavey were something feathered and improbable. Seavey's doubts—embarassed, harried—withdrew inside him.

Everything he saw on Johanna astonished Seavey. The cattle on the hillsides—humped, dangling dewlaps—

were no bigger than donkeys. The sheep and goats were scrawny and indistinguishable. The Johannese walked in twos and threes and discoursed, the extravagant arms of their cloaks flapping purposelessly in the trade wind. No man who was not a slave seemed to work.

The mountains above the town, which had been invisible from the missionary ship, rose steep and green. The tallest peak was said to hold an active volcano that bubbled colored muds the islanders used to fashion an intricate and brilliant pottery. While they waited for the boat that was to take them to Africa and the river station, the missionaries devoted themselves to natural history. Procter was a torrent of energy, chasing butterflies, pressing flowers, while Simpson, the youngest of the group, used his gun to preserve samples of the birds. Seavey studied insects. He walked the steeper hillsides, through dug fields, and felt the muscles of his legs knitting again, secured to land. An unseen servant of Abdallah's had plaited for him a straw hat the color of English cream to replace the one of ship's canvas that was now too hot. The rim left a band of sweat on Seavey's high forehead that he wiped clean with his handkerchief. The sun's light was so intense that it made the threads of white cotton gleam as if the cloth were woven of a pliant crystal.

Lying against the hillsides, the handkerchief over his face, Seavey became convinced that he could feel the earth underneath him as he had felt the shift of ocean waters on his voyage out. The movements were slower, but no less insistent. He imagined the runs of molten rock that led to the volcano, the streams of fresh water that fed from the mountains, a blood of pure water behind the island's skin that sustained Johanna against the salt sea. He felt he was riding the island like a child riding an elephant.

The difficulty was that he had no way of talking to the elephant. He tried to think of the island as a self—not a god, of course, still a created thing—but a soul of a higher, larger order than man's: an intermediate order of being. Johanna the island, like the sea, like Britain before, though he had never known it, was an angel. This was what angels were—mute islands, mountains, seas. The earth was full of angels, but angels with whom he could not speak. For weeks, as the missionaries' journey to the coast was prepared, Seavey wandered on the hillsides, dreamt of seraphs, and stared at small things. He watched spiders, seeking refuge from the sun, in the corners of his room. Then, at evening, the shutters open, the wind from the sea blew everything clear.

As a special favor, the Prince Abdallah permitted the missionaries to visit his wives. "I doubt they will be beautiful," Procter told Seavey, "but we must do our duty." Seavey was excited at the prospect, eager to see women who, if not quite white, were almost so, ladies of breeding with whom he could laugh and converse.

Yet even as the men entered the palace, rising a few steps from the street, he sensed a slipping away. His eyes had difficulty with the alternation of light and dark, the cool corridors and the whitewashed spaces open to the sun. When the Englishmen reached the harem the Prince's wives and mother presented each missionary with a gift of nut cake covered with beaten silver foil. They gave the men a recipe for the sweet and talked of the climate. The prince's mother recited the names of the shipwrecked Scottish ladies who had tutored her son's wives in their language.

Seavey was surprised to see Procter take on an unaccustomed heartiness. The older man told jokes about small animals and made faces. He described his mother-in-law at length. At one point he squatted on the floor like a monkey and then sprang to his feet. Seavey tried to interrupt, but could not. Each time he started to speak it was as if Procter threw his massive body in the way, an arm swinging wide to complete one anecdote or start another. Gradually, Seavey's attention wandered. He watched the play of the fountain that stood in the center of the red-tiled courtyard and gazed at the soft, supple light which poured from the alabaster circles that topped each of the domes above the side-halls: a subsidiary light that made visible the central sunlight without being lost in it, the way the sound of the smaller channels of a waterfall is not lost in the rush of the main torrent, being pitched above it, free and distinct. The swirl of light muffled and distorted the conversation beside Seavey. It was as if he had forgotten the meaning of his own language. The play of brilliances seemed miraculous to him and made everything he heard alien, the words changed to the conversation of fishes.

"What surprised my mother," Abdallah told Seavey as they walked by the sea that evening, "is that the gentlemen seemed to have no interest in religion." The fishermen, phosphorescent scales dripping from their hands in the twilight, made signs of obeisance to the Prince as he passed. "She found it peculiar in missionaries"—the Prince fingered the garland about his neck—"but I told her you were different."

"But I'm not. In fact I'm worse than they are. I fear I have no urge to convert anyone anymore. I'm curious to see the Africans, but as to the fate of their souls, I'm afraid I'm indifferent." Seavey stopped in the sand, still warm from the day's heat. "I was curious about you as well, but I certainly don't want to convert you."

"Thank you. I don't want to convert you."

"I guess I'm not making myself clear. Since I came here I have felt an increasing isolation, but a contentment as well. It's why I asked you that question at Adams' dinner about the distances between God and men. I mean I'm happy talking to you now, here on this beach, but I feel I'd be equally content if you were dead."

Abdallah frowned. "Do you feel an urge to take life?"

"Not in the least. I just feel a certain self-sufficiency."

"Oh, that." The Prince clapped his hands and resumed walking. "I believe I've always felt that way. But then my father is a Sultan and I am a second son. I have many servants and no obligations. I can relax, indeed, I have to relax. My days are filled with reading and taking long walks. My sleep is important to me. I have seen, since my tenth birthday, some 3400 sunsets on this beach. Some days I was ill, of course, and couldn't come. I have perhaps another fifteen thousand to go. In all likelihood, when you have died of fever across the channel—which I don't wish for a moment, I hope you believe me—I will still be watching sunsets here." He turned toward Seavey and spread his delicate arms. "If Allah calls me to any purpose, I will be ready."

The Prince reached into a silken sack hidden in the folds of his cloak and turned back toward the Englishman. "Would you like a pomegranate?" he said. Seavey bit into the fruit and the cells and seeds confounded in his mouth.

In his mind's eye Seavey saw the rest of them leaving him on Johanna, their ship growing small in the sea. Its masts would bend over the horizon, thin dark lines dropping below the bright wash of water. He felt he was becoming a jewel of speculation, valuable to God perhaps, but worthless to his fellows—unmoving, thoughtful, useless. On an outing up the mountainside with Procter and Abdallah and his train, he imagined himself thrown into the whirlpool of a stream, slipping from the slender log that bridged it. He could see the Arab and the Englishman both leaping in after him, Procter rolling his sleeves, Abdallah tightening the belt that he wore around the middle of his cloak. Thrashing back and forth in the water, in and out of control, it seemed to Seavey that the two men were fighting each other to save him. At first he strove to deliver himself to Abdallah: their fingers touched then lost grip, the froth rushing between the tips. Then Seavey felt Procter's hand underneath his chin and Abdallah pulling at his legs, the two of them together dragging him from the torrent, heaving him on the ground. Above him, as the water poured from his nostrils, spouted from his mouth in a choking stream that burned the sides of his throat, Seavey saw the clearest, bluest, the most perfect imaginable heaven.

"You see, Arnold, the ground has shifted for me. I don' t relish the prospect of going over the water and preaching to anyone."

"Well you can't just walk out on us now."

"You misunderstand me, that's not my intention." Seavey reached for an offering, something he could give Procter to atone for his withdrawal. He did not want to displease the others or to trouble them. "Perhaps I could still accompany you in a menial capacity, like our Africans, as a carpenter or a cook?"

Procter pondered. "That might be a solution. You could dig latrines and teach the alphabet—teaching wouldn't contradict your scruples now, would it?" Taken with the idea, Procter rubbed his hands in glee, but the motion, slowed by the tropical heat, looked more as if he were rubbing a soothing lotion into them, healing an irritation of the sun. "I mean we won't be doing much else beside that ourselves for some time. We have to establish communication, to build trust before we can preach at any length. There'll be obstacles for all of us. That would be all right with you, wouldn't it?" Seavey saw a genuine concern in the other's face; he wanted things taken care of. "You could keep quiet, keep to yourself until you felt differently. I mean, it doesn't make any difference really, not for now, at least. You can think whatever you like."

"I should like that."

"Good. There's no need to leave you here, then."

"Were you thinking of that, then, of leaving me?"

"We couldn't have taken you by brute force, now could we?"

"No, you couldn't have."

And you wouldn't have been much use—Procter didn't say it, but Seavey was certain that was the real reason.

"Fine then." Procter clapped his arm around Seavey's shoulders.

"Tomorrow we sail. You won't miss your talks with the Arab now, will you?"

"No, I found them pleasant, but there's only so much that a foreigner can understand."

163

"Well then, we shan't tell him that part when we say goodbye."

Seavey appreciated the older man's political skill. He was beginning to enjoy the prospect of his own inconsequence. He felt comfortable with Procter, walking down the rocky path to the sea.

That evening Seavey packed for the final voyage. The accommodation he had made suited him. The work he would do would be a compensation, a payment to the others, for the pleasure that austerity would offer his own self. It was as if he had taken a vow of silence. He would be left alone.

A turn in the breeze blew Seavey's lantern out and he stepped through the door of Abdallah's villa. Alone, he sat down on a bench of rock and looked to the sky that burned above him. His English constellations had fled to the farthest northern horizon and there was such a swarm of new stars. He would have a lifetime in the Mission's new valley to search those strange skies. Yet in their totality, Seavey realized they were the same here as above the Equator, neither familiar nor alien: a stippled field of light across a black vault. It was only in excluding most of what they saw that Englishmen or Hottentots had appropriated an infinitesimal portion of the display and made it their own—a plough rather than a banner, a chair rather than a crown.

In their entirety, they were unassailable. Spread out,

there was no wholeness to them, but instead a random-
ness so vast, a chaos so powerful, it seemed to Seavey
only a God could have made it. Only in the smallest
parts was it amenable to the grasp of his mind. Each
time he tried to expand the range of his vision, nothing held for more than a second. He could not finish
a constellation without its exploding into something
else. The possible lines between the stars were endless:
a multitude of combination.

And still just a bowl of light. Seavey tried to see again
the English stars of his childhood, searched his mind
for the memory, then abandoned the quest. Who could
ever remember, he thought, the whole of a night sky?
Seavey closed his eyes, but the stars did not go away.

# Acknowledgments

The following stories previously appeared as noted:

"Our Big Game" – *North American Review,* Vol. 263, No. 4

"The Sauna After Ted's Funeral" – *Ascent,* Vol. 16, No. 2

"Mobley's Troubles" – *Ascent,* Vol. 5, No. 1

"On the Flats" – *Harper's,* Vol. 277, No. 1661

"A Good White Hunter" – *A Matter of Crime: New Stories from the Masters of Mystery and Suspense, Vol. 4* (New York: Harcourt Brace Jovanovich, 1988)

"A Second Language" – *Harvard Review,* Number Thirty Seven

"The Immanence of God in the Tropics" – *Yale Review,* Vol. 73, No. 4

# The Author

Photo by Barbara Gale

George Rosen, born in Chicago and educated at Harvard, was a Peace Corps Volunteer in Kenya, which served as the setting for *Black Money: A Novel of Modern Africa* (Scarborough House, 1990), called by *Kirkus Reviews* "a sophisticated, rich, and tantalizing portrait of East Africa" and by *Library Journal* "a strong study of power that corrupts at every level and of idealism that persists." His short stories have appeared in *Harper's*, the *Yale Review*, and the *Harvard Review*, among other magazines. As a freelance journalist, Rosen has reported on West Africa for the *Atlantic* and on Mexico for the *Boston Globe* and writes frequently for the *Globe*'s op-ed page. His awards include the Frank O'Connor Memorial Award and Fellowships from the Artists Foundation and the Massachusetts Cultural Council. He lives in Gloucester, Massachusetts.

## About the Type

This book was set in Minion. Designed for Adobe by Robert Slimbach, the Minion™ font is based on classical old-style types from the late Renaissance period, but was created with current technology in mind. Rigidly straight lines and sturdy strokes give the Minion font design a gracefulness that transcends the ages.

Designed by John Taylor-Convery
Composed at JTC Imagineering, Santa Maria, CA